Six-Gun TERRORS

AIRSHIP 27 PRODUCTIONS

Six-Gun Terrors Volume 3
© 2017 Fred Adams Jr.

Published by Airship 27 Productions
www.airship27.com
www.airship27hangar.com

Cover illustration © 2017 Ted Hammond
Interior illustrations © 2017 Art Cooper

Editor: Ron Fortier
Associate Editor: Gordon Dymowski
Marketing and Promotions Manager: Michael Vance
Production and design by Rob Davis.

ISBN-10: 1-946183-27-X
ISBN-13: 978-1-946183-27-9

Printed in the United States of America

10 9 8 7 6 5 4 3 2 1

VOLUME THREE
FRED ADAMS JR.

THE SLITHERING TERROR

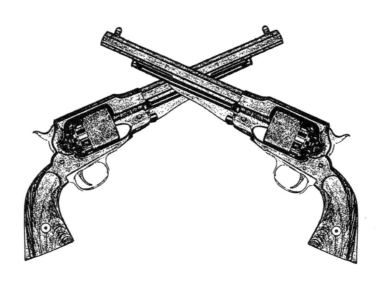

I

Ed Durst spat into the fire. "I still say we maybe should'a stayed with the Diamond Blaze outfit. By the time we meet up with Ketchum in Denver, we won't have two bits left between us."

"I didn't hold no knife to your throat when we left." Hank Martin leaned forward and grabbed the handle of the campfire coffee pot. He poured the last of it into his battered tin cup, took a drink, then wiped his moustache with his shirtsleeve. "You said yourself you couldn't take any more guff from Bob Simmons. I figure we stayed on long enough, we'd be drawing straws to see who got to shoot him first."

"I'd say that's about right." Durst levered himself into a standing position. He stretched and yawned. "Sure is quiet out here. And dark."

"Won't be dark for long." Hank pointed at the edge of the Moon rising over the distant ridge. "It's almost full tonight. That ought to brighten things up a little."

"You sure Ketchum'll get us on with his crew?"

"If he don't, my sister'll give him six kinds of hell and make him sleep in the barn. Even so, there's always another cattle drive or another ranch. Work is where you find it."

"Yeah, that's so. But I'll still feel better with a little more money in my billfold."

Hank finished his coffee and dumped the grounds from his cup. "You worry too much about money, Ed. When's the last time you ran dry?"

He grinned. "That night in Barstow when I took up with that little dance hall girl. I gave her my last nickel for one more kiss."

Hank snickered. "For that much money, I hope you got to pick the spot where she kissed you."

That got them both laughing. Hank was rolling a cigarette when the horses started neighing. They were pawing at the ground, nervous.

"What's spooked the horses?"

"Guess we better find out." Hank picked up his Winchester and turned his back on the campfire, eyes searching the darkness beyond. He stepped away from the fire with Ed close behind.

"Probably a coyote," Ed said, sliding his Colt from the holster.

"Maybe a two-legged one. That or a puma, though I never knew one to range this far from the mountains.

The horses were tethered to a pair of scrub trees about twenty yards from the fire. Hank could see their wide eyes shining in the flickering glow. Hank's bay Tumble and Ed's paint Tommy Boy were taking nervous, mincing steps side to side. Their neighing sounded almost piteous, fearful.

"I never seen horses act like that before," said Ed, taking Tommy Boy's head in the crook of his arm and stroking his brow. "Easy, fella."

The curve of the Moon crept over the ridge like a big turnip watch working its way out of a vest pocket. Hank strained his eyes, looking one way then another.

"Damned if I can see anything."

Then they heard it, a dry swishing over the sand like somebody dragging a sack of feed in a slalom path. Then a whirring sound like a windlass spinning free.

The horses whinnied, and Tommy Boy reared, breaking loose from his tether and pulling Ed around as Tumbler bolted past him. Ed stared over Hank's shoulder. "Mother of God!"

Hank spun to look into a pair of glowing golden eyes two feet higher than his own, bobbing like a balloon in the darkness. He levered a shell into the chamber and fired, although he probably missed the target by two feet in his panic.

A pair of leathery arms ending in taloned hands reached for him as he fired again. A thick coil whipped around his legs and pulled him off his feet. His rifle flew across the clearing.

Hank was pinned to the ground as the eyes came closer to his own and he saw the pupils were diamond slits. A forked tongue slithered out of an impossibly wide mouth and slathered his face with numbing slime.

Ed had run from the creature, desperately shouting for Tommy Boy, praying he could jump on his horse and escape the horror. He stopped suddenly. In the moonlight he saw a handful of saguaros he hadn't noticed before. Behind him, Hank screamed in terror.

The dark shapes began to move, and Ed realized that the monster wasn't alone. One of the intruders, a wizened old man with a shock of white hair began keening in a strange language. Ed turned to run, but rough hands seized his arms and dragged him through the scrub back toward his now silent friend.

The old man spoke in an unknown tongue, and the braves who had captured Durst threw him to the ground. He kicked and fought all the more as the creature slithered toward him. The shaman nodded and the snake head hovered over his face. The tongue painted his skin with its ooze. Ed's face went numb, and he felt himself sliding down a dark hole into unconsciousness.

II

Durken squinted in the yellow light of the kerosene lamp as he worked the awl through the stiff leather of his chaps. Bill Slye walked past on his way into the bunkhouse and snickered. "You need to get you a wife to sew that for you. By the time you get done, it's gonna look like you done it, Durken." Slye bit a quid from his twist of tobacco and chewed it lazily as he admired Durken's handiwork.

"I'd be scared to marry a woman strong enough to push an awl through this leather. And as for my sewing skill, one more wise crack from you, Slye, and I'll stitch your mouth shut, and there won't be no mistake who did it."

Slye laughed and sauntered through the bunkhouse door where a noisy poker game was in progress.

Durken bit off a length of the waxed thread and tied off his stitches. Doc Chambers rode out to the ranch from Bacon Rock three days before to put a few to match in his thigh where a buffalo had wheeled around in a stampede and gored him. Durken had been sitting around the bunkhouse ever since, healing up, and he'd probably need another two or three days before he could ride right again.

It seemed every time he got himself hurt, it took a little bit longer to recover. The last time he shaved, he saw the salt was gradually winning the battle over the pepper in his drooping moustache. Maybe Slye was right, and maybe he should marry Maggie, the Triple Six Ranch's stout Irish cook and settle down once and for all, but some men just weren't cut out for hearth and home. Durken was one of them.

He looked across the hard packed yard and saw a lanky shape strolling from the direction of the Big House, "The Mansion," Homer Eldridge, the owner of the Triple Six liked to call it. It was McAfee, Durken's friend and cohort in one scrape after another since the days they rode as scouts for Sherman in the March to the Sea.

"Clean shirt and a fresh shave. Looks to me you've been over to see Miss Sarah." Although not yet official, it was pretty much acknowledged that McAfee and Sarah, Eldridge's daughter would be married someday, if Eldridge could ever bring himself to accept the idea.

"Maybe you oughta sign up with the Pinkertons, your skill at deduction being what it is." McAfee stepped into the angle of light that shone through the bunkhouse doorway. He grinned. "Looks like you're getting ready to put your armor back on." McAfee was an inch or so shorter than Durken and cobbled together from the same mix of sinew, bone and barbed wire. Unlike Durken, he was clean shaven, since his moustache grew out like straws in a broom.

Durken stood a little slower than he was used to doing. "Let's see what kind of job I did." He leaned his backside against the clapboards of the building and bent his injured leg at the knee to tie he chaps onto it.

"Not bad." McAfee plopped into a chair beside Durken. "Though I'd bet Maggie'd done a neater job of it."

Durken snorted. "Maggie's a cooker not a sewer. Maybe you can get Miss Sarah to crochet you a new pair, or stitch a daisy on your old ones."

"That buff had a damned sharp horn to go through your chaps and your leg too. I figure by now your hide's as tough as that leather."

"Well, he won't do that again. What's that saying you like to quote? 'Time and chance happen to them all'? Where's that from, Proverbs?"

"The right book and the wrong book: Ecclesiastes." He studied the palm sized patch. "Using a chunk of that buff's hide to patch the rip is a nice touch. Sort of a new twist on 'hair of the dog.'"

Durken and McAfee had been riding point on a buffalo hunt with Homer Eldridge, who was entertaining some of his rich friends from San Francisco with a little bit of adventure. McAfee had scouted a herd moving through, and led the entourage nearly twenty miles to a likely place the herd would pass. Ever the ostentatious host, Eldridge brought not only his friends, but a half dozen of the crew to put up a pavilion tent, and Charlie Ming, the crew cook with the chuck wagon the working men used on cattle drives.

Eldridge brought Eli Ross, vice-president of the Bank of San Francisco, State Senator Charles Manhammer, and wealthy importer Samuel Jeffries, among others. In all, nine would-be buffalo hunters comprised the party.

"Ain't that bunch of nabobs a sight?" Harley Wilcox said, eyeing the gentlemen's club. "All of 'em dressed right out of a dime novel. No question which is us and which is them." None of the hunting party but Eldridge wore a stitch of clothing that was older than a week: dungarees, gingham shirts, and kerchiefs topped with ten-gallon hats. "You reckon we'll have to show them which end of the rifle the bullet comes out of?"

"Naah," said Durken, shaking his head. "I'm betting those boys have shot a lot of skeet in their time. Oh hell, here comes Eldridge."

Homer Eldridge wore a tan suit with a waist-length jacket and riding pants with suede grip panels sewn to the inner thighs. He rode Dandy, his chestnut stallion, toward the knot of cowboys like a Roman emperor. "Are you boys ready to go?"

"Yep," said Durken. "We'll take you to them. The herd's three miles that way," he pointed east.

McAfee, Wilcox, and Durken saddled up, and the four rode across the brittle grassland until they topped a rise and could see the buffalo on the plain below. The herd was small, relatively speaking. Packs of buffalo skinners had decimated the great herds by their indiscriminate and wasteful slaughter, stripping off the hides, cutting out the tongues, and leaving the carcasses to rot by the thousand.

Eldridge opened a telescope and put it to his eye, appraising the buffalo as he would cattle at an auction. A big bull, the undisputed master of the herd was the prize of the hunt.

"That one," Eldridge said, and he handed Durken his telescope. "That bull," his eyes glittered with excitement. "I want his head on the wall." Eldridge's study had one wall covered with his collection of exotic guns, and another covered with the heads and hides of every animal that lived in the territory, plus a few that didn't.

Durken studied the buffalo for a moment. He was bigger than average; as tall as Durken's bay Thunder, he surely carried a ton of meat on his ten-foot frame. He was a magnificent beast, and Durken thought that it was a shame that a Henry repeater made him prey for a sawed-off runt like Eldridge. "I'll see what I can do."

"They're grazing right now," said McAfee, "so this would be a good time for an approach."

"I've thought about that," said Eldridge, "and I don't think it would be as exciting for my friends as it would if you ran them past the camp and they could shoot from the bluff."

"Like a shooting gallery in a carnival," said Wilcox with a grin, which earned him a withering stare from Eldridge.

"The herd's not a big one," said McAfee, "a hundred, maybe a hundred twenty head. The smaller herd will likely run past faster, especially if they hang in a group, and give your party less time to shoot. Also, because the herd is smaller, they maneuver quicker. They don't exactly think like cattle. It might be a trick to get them to run by there the way you want."

"Well, that's how I want it."

"There's one other issue," said Durken. "Your friends are gonna shoot into that herd, likely hit more than a few, but they're gonna miss some too. I think I speak for all of us when I say that I don't want to catch a .50 caliber slug from a bad shot, and I sure as hell don't want my horse hit."

Eldridge opened his mouth to speak, but McAfee cut him off. "There's a way to manage that, I think. Have one of the men drive a stake two hundred yards out as a marker. We peel off at the stake, and you and your friends don't shoot at anything 'til we pull away. Durken? Harley?"

"Sounds sensible," said Durken. Wilcox nodded his agreement.

McAfee pulled his watch from his vest pocket. "It's a little after two o'clock now. Will you be ready by three?"

Eldridge nodded. "Three would be good."

"We'll start a few minutes earlier and have the herd arrive just like the Kansas City Express."

"All right, then, get to it."

Durken spoke up. "Do your friends know where to shoot?"

Eldridge blinked. "What?"

"Maybe I should've said where to aim. Do they know where to aim to bring down a buffalo on the first shot...make it a clean kill?" Eldridge looked uncertain, so Durken went on, "Tell them to aim behind the buff's shoulder where the fur is thinner than the shag around his head. Then settle on a target area about a third of the way down from the backbone. The muscles aren't as thick, and they're less likely to hit a rib."

Eldridge snorted and spurred his horse, riding away in a huff.

McAfee took a key from his vest pocket and wound his watch. "You just can't help yourself, can you?"

Durken shook his head. "Nope."

McAfee, Durken, Wilcox, and Marty Hamer waited for a while, watching the buffalo.

"That's a pitiful small herd compared to some I saw as a boy," said Hamer. Once I sat on a knoll and watched for a half an hour before they was all past."

"I hear General Sherman had herd after herd hunted down and killed to starve the Indians," Wilcox said. "Between the Army and the railroaders, they've about wiped them out." In his prosecution of the "Indian situation," using a gambit reminiscent of his infamous March to the Sea, William Tecumseh Sherman authorized the mass killing of the buffalo to starve resistant tribes into submission and force them off desirable land.

McAfee said, "I read once in some book a professor said that if people on the moon looked through a telescope there were two things they could pick out, that big wall in China and herds of buffalo running on the plains."

"He said there were people on the moon?" Hamer said, incredulous.

"No, you fool, if there were. If."

Durken rolled his eyes. "Maybe we oughta send you both to the Moon and you can report back on the subject; that is, if the Moon men don't eat you for supper."

McAfee checked his watch. "Quarter of three. Time to start the show."

The cowboys closed in on the rear of the herd, riding slowly and quietly. The buffalo were moving at a leisurely pace, more or less in the direction the cowboys wanted them to go. The men fanned out into a vee. Durken pulled his bandanna over the bridge of his nose to keep out some of the dust.

On McAfee's signal the cowboys came up alongside the herd and spooked it with shouts and gunfire. Soon the herd was at a dead run. The riders stayed to the outside. If their intention was to simply run the herd, they could have fallen away, but to maneuver it into the gun sights of Eldridge's party, they had to hang with the chase.

What the herd lacked in number was compensated by the tidal wave of sheer force the stampede represented. Outside the herd, the buffalo were less a hazard to the cowboys than the uneven terrain. They all prayed that none of the horses would step into a chuckhole or stumble on a rock. Ahead, Durken saw the marker, a four-foot post with a streaming red cloth dancing in the breeze.

Durken and Wilcox were turning the herd to give a clear shot to the waiting hunters when the bull made an executive decision to go another way. He cut to the outside and collided side to side with Thunder. Thunder staggered to the right but kept his footing. If he hadn't, he and Durken would have been crushed under the hooves of the following herd.

The bull wheeled and swung its head hard right, plunging its horn into Durken's leg. Durken bellowed in pain. Unable to swing his rifle around, he pulled his Colt and put two bullets through the buffalo's eye and out the other side of its head. The bull fell away, taking a bloody gobbet of Durken's thigh with him.

Durken yanked the reins and Thunder peeled away from the herd. He stopped fifty yards further, and Durken unceremoniously fell from the saddle. He heard the crack of rifle fire, barely audible over the pounding hooves of the herd. His last conscious thought was, I thought the war was over.

McAfee stood over Durken. "Get his chaps off him and cut open his trousers. He started undoing his fly.

Hamer gaped. "What the hell are you going to do?"

"See that he doesn't get lockjaw."

III

"**A**ll things considered, it's better he got me and not Thunder. Thunder wasn't wearing chaps."

"Yeah. That bull might've caught him between his bones and done him in. You're lucky too that he didn't break your leg. You know, Eldridge is still pissed at you for ruining the trophy head." The exit wounds left very little of the buffalo's face to mount. "The first shot would've finished the buff. Why'd you shoot him twice?"

"'Cause I only had two bullets left in the gun. As for Eldridge, I think he's more exercised that I shot the bull in front of his friends instead of him shooting it. That and you pouring half a bottle of his fancy Irish whiskey over my thigh to disinfect it. You really didn't need to. I hear Hamer damn near fainted when you pissed on my leg. Of course he wasn't in the war to see that every day."

"Next time, maybe Eldridge can ride point, see what it's all about firsthand."

"Cold day in hell."

"Yep."

"Here comes Maggie."

Durken shucked out of his chaps but didn't sit down. Maggie was bustling across the darkened yard swinging a small iron pot by its handle. The stout red-haired Irishwoman loved Durken with all her heart, as he did her with all of his. The problem was, neither of them could figure out what to do about it.

"On your feet again, are you?" she snapped. "When'll you learn to do what you're told, you scallawag?"

"Aw, Maggie, I'm just being polite. Ain't a man supposed to stand up when a lady comes by?" He turned to McAfee and swatted him with his hat. "Where's your manners? On your feet."

"Don't give me none of yer sass, Durken, or I'll feed your meal to the hounds."

He sat down in his chair, the picture of mock contrition. "Yes, ma'am. What's in the kettle?"

"Tonight, Himself and his friends are all enjoying that buffalo you killed, and though he'd hang my head on the wall if he knew I brought this, I thought it was only right that you got to eat some of it too. There's a piece of flank in there and some carrots and potatoes and greens."

"Thanks, Maggie. That's awful nice of you."

Her brow creased with irritation. "Someday, Durken, you'll learn to not mix a compliment with an insult."

"They call that an 'oxymoron'," McAfee said. "I read that once in some book."

"Well you got the last half right for sure," Maggie said, a fist on her hip. She handed the kettle to Durken and blushed when his hand closed over hers around the handle. "I'll come back for the pot tomorrow," she said, a little less pepper in her voice. "Good evening, McAfee. Good night, Durken."

The cowboys both said goodnight, Maggie gave a little curtsey, and she started back toward the Mansion.

"Why don't you just marry her and get it over with, Durken?"

"The same reason you don't marry Miss Sarah. It'd disrupt the natural order of things."

And to that, McAfee had no reply. They sat on the porch of the bunkhouse for a while. Durken turned down the lamp so the moths would go elsewhere. Inside, the poker game broke up, and Smeck took up his guitar and started singing a plaintive song about a doomed gunslinger named Devil Johnny. Finally, McAfee spoke. "Been quiet around here for a while pretty much, ain't it?"

"Yep."

"But it never seems to last."

"Nope."

"Damn."

"Yep."

IV

For the next two days, Wilcox continued in Durken's place as co-foreman with McAfee, and Durken busied himself cleaning his guns, sharpening his knives, and repairing his tack. That and sipping whiskey from a flask the whole day to keep the edge off the burning pain in his thigh. Eldridge had a no-drinking rule on the ranch, but he didn't have either the heart or the nerve to call Durken out on it. Sitting around frustrated him, but Durken knew the more he used the leg now, the longer it would be before he could ride again.

He was replacing a buckle on his saddle in the early morning chill when he saw two men on horseback in the distance. He picked up an ornate pair of binoculars fitted in brass and silver, a gift from the General, and took a good look at the approaching strangers. Before he knew who they were, he knew what they were. Men in vested suits under dusters, one wearing a short-brimmed Stetson and the other a bowler; they were either Pinkertons or Federal agents.

When they came a little closer, Durken raised the glasses again. The man in the derby was Willis Tate, Special Agent for the United States Secret Service. Durken cursed under his breath. "Charlie!"

In a few seconds a short Chinese man in overalls and a striped shirt made from a mattress tick came outside, Charlie Ming, the crew cook. "What you need, Durken?"

Durken lowered his glasses and spoke, never taking his eyes off the riders. "Would you please bring out my ten-gauge, a couple of shells, and an oil rag? I'd get them myself, but I don't want to take my eyes off those two."

"Sure thing, Durken." Charlie disappeared into the bunkhouse and came back with a wicked sawed-off double-barreled shotgun. Durken cracked it open and loaded both barrels. He laid the gun open-breeched across his lap and thumbed back both hammers, then he set to wiping the barrel and works with the rag. He kept his head down but watched the agents from beneath the brim of his hat.

Durken and McAfee had an antagonistic history with Agent Willis Tate. They had been drafted by the General to track down a murderous pack of renegades, and when Red Hawk and the Cat Warriors turned out to be more than a simple native tribe, the Secret Service stuck its snout in the trough. They had been forced into the traces alongside Tate and his crew of ex-Pinkerton mercenaries and Tate had nearly gotten them all killed. It was a story Durken and McAfee still weren't allowed to tell, and maybe never would be.

To Durken and McAfee, Tate represented everything that was bad about the government; unbridled authority welded to irresponsible ego, though they might not put it in exactly those words. Tate's sudden appearance could mean nothing but trouble. Durken was glad McAfee wasn't around; he was glad to handle Tate on his own and in a mood for it. Besides that, McAfee was just too damned diplomatic.

Tate and his companion stopped ten feet short of the bunkhouse. Both had their dusters pulled back exposing cross-draw holsters, a fact not lost on Durken. "Elrod Durken." A statement not a question, it had the tone of a challenge. Apparently Tate hadn't learned much from their last encounter.

"Special Agent Willis Tate," Durken answered in kind. His eyes rose slowly and locked on the agent's. "Who's your friend?"

Tate tilted his derby to the left. "This is Agent Royster Black."

"How come he ain't 'special'?"

Tate had a humorless smile that showed only the edges of his teeth and barely bent the perfectly straight line of his clipped moustache. "He's new to the Service."

Durken spoke without taking his eyes off Tate's. "Agent Black, I bet Special Agent Tate here never told you what a special job he did out in the Sierras." Durken leaned on the word "special." "Got his men killed and damn near died himself because he thought he knew and we didn't. And now he's foolish enough to ride in here ready to pull down on me after he's seen firsthand what I do. This scatter gun's right comprehensive. I figure both barrels at once'd take down both of you, both your horses, and those three calves in the pen across the yard."

From the corner of his eye, Durken saw Black's eyes twitch toward Tate.

"Too bad your breech is open, Durken. You could never close that gun, cock the hammers, and pull the triggers faster than we can draw."

Durken smiled grimly, still staring down Tate. "See, Black? Tate doesn't know what he doesn't know. This gun's a Mackenzie. Those Scottie boys made it so you can cock it while it's open." Durken moved his thumb to reveal the hammers at full ride. All I have to do is snap her shut, and you'll both be a pile of guts."

"One of us will get you, Durken."

"Maybe." He paused."Charlie!" Tate and Black heard the ratchet of a shell jacked into a Winchester. The barrel poked through an open window. "You see, Black, he really doesn't know what he doesn't know. I bet the two of you watched the crew ride out and figured I'd be here all by myself, didn't you, Black?" Black didn't answer, and Durken knew he was right. "Pick one, Charlie."

"The one on the right."

"He goes for his gun, kill him. Now Agent Black, you are," he paused, "special too. Well Tate? Now it's down to you and me."

Tate flushed and looked away. "Oh this is foolishness. I have a communique for you and McAfee from General Sherman."

"Is that so? Where is it?"

"My inside coat pocket."

"Agent Black, hold your reins with your gun hand and reach across with your other. Take out the letter. Don't get any ideas about Tate's pistol. Charlie don't shoot as good as me, but this close he can't miss."

Black did as he was told and in a moment held a white envelope between his thumb and forefinger.

"Drop it on the ground." He did. "McAfee and I'll read it when he gets back here. Now, turn your horses around and ride out. If you're smart, you won't come back."

"You know, Durken, threatening a Federal agent is a felony."

"Then arrest me. Right here, right now." Durken chuckled. "You wouldn't be here if somebody didn't need McAfee and me for some dirty work. And I sure as hell can't do anybody much good in a jail cell. You won't arrest me, no more than you'd'a shot me, Tate, 'cause you got *orders*. Now I'm giving you one. Haul your ass out of here."

Tate and Black wheeled their horses. Durken snapped the shotgun shut. Tate's back stiffened. "That's right, Tate. I closed the breech. Now ride. And don't turn around, or you'll think Lot's wife got off easy." Neither Durken nor Charlie moved until Tate and Black were out the gate and headed down the road toward Bacon Rock.

"Thanks, Charlie. You're a good friend." Durken rose slowly to his feet and hobbled toward the letter lying on the ground.

"I could do no less. You've taken my part more than once."

Durken picked up the envelope and stared at it. "Unless I'm wrong, we might be doing it again real soon."

He was still on the porch with the Mackenzie across his lap when McAfee came back with the crew in the late afternoon. "What's Eldridge got you doing now, scaring off bill collectors?"

Durken shook his head. "Nope. You and I had a visitor today, and I'm making sure he doesn't come back." McAfee's eye squinted in that odd of way if his when he was puzzled. Durken spat a stream of tobacco juice. "Special Agent Willis Tate."

McAfee's face darkened. "That son of a whore. What'd he want?"

Durken slid the envelope from the pocket of his shirt. "To deliver this. He says it's from the General."

"Well what's it say?"

"I ain't read it yet. It's addressed to us both. I decided to be polite and wait for you." He handed it to McAfee who turned it over and pointed to a curved mark on the front.

"What's this, the new Capital postmark?"

"Nope. That's the hoof print of Tate's horse. The situation got a little... tense is a good word."

"You know what this probably means, don't you?"

"We don't hear from the General 'less he needs something done."

Durken and McAfee had served as scouts for General Sherman during the March to the Sea, and after the war, they drifted into range work and Sherman was put in charge of the "Indian situation" in the western territories to get him from under the feet of Grant's administration.

When he needed their skills as scouts and trackers, Sherman never hesitated to reconscript the pair into the Army's service. As the General once said, "If I were on the run, you two are the last men I'd want chasing my bony ass."

"Pandora's Box," said McAfee, staring at the letter. "I hate to open it. Who knows what evils are going to fly out?"

"As I recall the story, she had a choice. We don't. If we don't open that letter soon, it's gonna open itself."

McAfee slit the envelope with his Case knife. In it was a single sheet of foolscap with a handwritten message. He read it aloud. "'Durken and McAfee, I am in need of your skills. Meet me at the rail siding three miles east of Bacon Rock tomorrow morning. William Tecumseh Sherman.'"

"I guess we better go and find out what's going on."

"We?" McAfee pointed to Durken's leg. "You can't ride yet. I'll go myself and tell you all about it later."

"The hell you will. Who said anything about riding a horse? We'll... what's that word the General uses? Requisition? We'll requisition the buckboard. I need to get off this chair and go someplace else for a while anyway."

McAfee ran his thumbnail along the stubble on his chin. "What concerns me is having Tate back in our lives again."

"He rode out here with his holster clear, all bluster like he was planning to ride me off in leg irons, but I knew he wasn't serious about it."

"How do you know that?"

"Because he didn't bring a dozen more agents and a Gatling gun with him."

"Well, there's no love lost between him and the General. Whatever this is all about, it must be important to put those two back in the same yoke."

"You better be the one to tell Eldridge. He's still snorting fire at me over that buffalo."

McAfee chuckled. "I think I'll wait 'til after supper, long about the time he's letting his food settle."

"I don't know a man more deserving."

V

McAfee crossed the yard with mixed feelings. There were few things he liked less than delivering bad news to Homer Eldridge, but a visit to the Mansion meant he'd get to see the pretty green-eyed, honey-haired Sarah. The Mansion. McAfee snorted at the pretension of the name Eldridge gave the rambling, ornate Gothic house with its turrets, balconies, and fancy gingerbread trim, an exact copy, Eldridge boasted, of the home of the wealthiest shipping magnate in San Francisco. It might be fashionable in Frisco, thought McAfee, but out here it fits like a whorehouse in a churchyard.

He stepped onto the wide porch and raised his fist to knock on the door. Before he could, it swung open and Miss Sarah slipped out. Before he could speak, she put a finger to her lips. She pulled the door closed behind her and stood on tip toes to give McAfee a kiss. "I figured I'd better do that now. If you're here to see Father, I probably won't get the chance later. How do you like my new dress?" She turned around and McAfee whistled.

The dress was yellow gingham with flounces and ruffles in all the right places. Sarah made some dresses for herself with bustles, but McAfee liked it better when she made one like this that flattered her natural figure. "Sure is pretty, Sarah, but you'd make a gunny sack look good."

McAfee took off his hat and stood awkwardly turning it by the brim in his fingers. "I have to talk to the boss. Durken and I have to go to see the General tomorrow."

Sarah shook her head slowly side to side. "Oh, Clarence, not again. Why do you have to go?"

McAfee could no more tell her about the missions that he and Durken carried out for Sherman than he could tell anyone, because they were "classified." "Because when Durken and I go, we make sure that life stays safe for you, Maggie, your father, and everybody else we know and care about. I wouldn't trust that job to anybody else."

"I understand that, but it doesn't make it easier for me when you go."

"But I always come back."

She smiled. "Yes you do, and I love you for it."

The door cracked open and Maggie stuck her head out. "Himself says when you two are done mooning over each other, he'll be waiting in his study."

The intrusion broke the mood, and Sarah and McAfee laughed as they entered the foyer of the Mansion. "What the devil is that?" McAfee pointed up the stairs to a shining man-sized figure standing with mailed fists on the pommel of a broadsword.

"Something new Father brought back from his last trip to San Francisco. It's a full suit of armor from the Tenth Century. German, I think, maybe French. He can give you its whole pedigree."

"I guess it'll come in handy if a dragon ever attacks the Triple Six, but a .45 would turn that tin can into a sieve. What's he gonna do next? Dig a moat around the place?"

Down the hallway, the door to Eldridge's study swung open and Eldridge stepped into the hall. "Get in here, McAfee. I don't have all night."

"Yes, sir. I'm on my way."

Sarah gave his hand a squeeze and she whispered, "I'll wait outside under the big ash tree." She gave him another squeeze and she was gone.

When McAfee entered Eldridge's study, he found him seated behind a mahogany banker's desk big enough to serve eight people dinner. He was dressed, as he usually was around the Triple Six, in the garb of the "gentleman rancher," a vest over a starched shirt with a wing collar and a silk stock. He prided himself on working with his brain instead of his back. It must be hard work, McAfee thought, because Eldridge was bald past the crown of his head. To compensate, he kept a full beard so that if he shut his mouth and painted lips on his brow, you could turn his head upside down and it would look no less normal.

"What the devil is that?"

"Close the door, McAfee." Eldridge leaned back in his chair and folded his hands across his stomach. "What is it you need to see me about?"

"Mister Eldridge, Durken and I got a letter from the General today, and…"

"Damn him!" Eldridge slammed his palms on the desk, rattling the lid of his humidor. "What makes that man think he can just whistle for you two and I have to disrupt the operation of this place while he sends you off to who knows where? And you can't even tell me why."

"No, sir, I can't. So far, I don't know yet myself. We have to meet with him tomorrow."

"I suppose Durken's perfectly fit to ride now, after he's sat around on my payroll for almost a week."

"No, sir, to tell the truth, I was going to ask if we could take the buckboard, since Durken can't go on horseback just yet."

Eldridge fumed. He knew from past experience that bucking the General's authority was like arguing with a wolverine. "And while you're traipsing all over hell's half acre, who's going to run the place?"

"I'd suggest Harley Wilcox. He's been riding with me instead of Durken this week, and he has a good handle on things."

"All right. When you leave here, send Wilcox over. And I'll expect you back on the job as soon this adventure is finished."

McAfee nodded. "Wild horses couldn't keep me away, Mister Eldridge."

Eldridge's brow darkened as he caught the drift of McAfee's comment. He opened his mouth to say something then closed it again and swiveled his chair to show McAfee his back. "Close the door on your way out."

Outside, McAfee found Sarah waiting as she promised. "I don't have to ask if he's angry."

"Let's just say he's consistent."

"How long will you be gone?"

"Whoa, whoa. I don't even know if we are going anywhere. We're just going to meet with the General tomorrow."

"Well I know," she said, her eyes blazing. "Every time Sherman calls you, one of you or both of you ends up with stitches, gunshot wounds, and broken bones. This time won't be any different."

"Yes, it will. Durken can't ride. The General needs us both or he wouldn't have asked for us both. If he can't go, we can't go. Just wait 'til tomorrow. Then we'll know for sure."

Sarah buried her face in McAfee's shoulder and he felt hot tears soaking through his shirt. They stood that way for a long time, and finally, McAfee took her face in his hands and kissed her gently. "I always come back, Sarah. I always come back."

Sarah nodded and turned away, walking with her head down back to the Mansion. For the first time he could remember, McAfee fought back the salt sting of a tear of his own.

VI

Durken climbed stiffly onto the buckboard as McAfee tied Sweetheart's reins to the rail of the wagon. The Appaloosa's saddle and all of McAfee's gear were loaded in the back of the buckboard so that he could leave immediately from Bacon Rock if he had to, and Durken could bring back the buckboard.

As they rode through the gate, McAfee looked over his shoulder at the Mansion and saw a curtain move in an upstairs window. Sarah was no fool. She knew from that moment that she might never see him again.

"They make it tough, don't they?" Durken said, twitching the reins and picking up the pace as the buckboard rattled down the rutted road. "The women, I mean. Maggie read me the Riot Act when she can see I can't ride a horse to save my life."

"There are days when I think we were both better off before we met those two."

"Life was simpler, that's for sure, but trying to keep life the same forever is like trying to hold smoke in your fingers. You just ride the horse every day and see what shows up around the next bend."

"Do you ever think about settling down?"

"Sure I do, then I remind myself that I'm a saddle tramp at heart. I truly don't think it would work for me; maybe for you, but I don't think I could live that way for the rest of my days. Remember what I said last night about the natural order of things? No doubt in my mind that I love Maggie dearly, but I love her the way things are."

His brow creased in thought."What's that poem about the urn you like so much, the one by that guy died of consumption?"

"You mean Keats. 'Ode on a Grecian Urn.'"

"I guess that's the one; the lovers always reaching for each other but never quite getting there. The only way they can touch each other is to break the urn...like I said, upset the order of things. I marry Maggie, I won't change, and I'd bet you wouldn't change a hair either if you married Miss Sarah. But they will." Durken turned his head and saw McAfee staring at him. "What?"

"All these years I read things to you that I read, and I think it rolls off you like rain from an otter, and then you come out with a thought like that. Jesus."

Durken shrugged. "Sometimes it's like riding through a nettle patch and picking up little prickly things you carry around with you, and one day you notice one when it pokes through your trouser cuff."

McAfee was silent for a moment then said, "Of course there is one other way to look at that urn. Folks put dead men's ashes in them."

They rolled into Bacon Rock around ten o'clock. Two streets of one-and two-story clapboard buildings that the right combination of fire and wind could wipe out in an hour. The town was never bustling like, say, Denver or Reno, but it was busy enough most days. Shops were open, people were walking up and down the plank sidewalks, and horses were tethered at the hitching rails.

"Before we surrender ourselves to the will of the U. S. Army, what do you say we stop at the Silver Dollar for a whiskey?" said Durken. "Might be our last chance for a while."

"Good idea. Even if we do have another chance after lunch."

The Silver Dollar was dark and cool inside. Bobby Lee, Liam's hired man was sweeping a day's worth of beer soaked sawdust and peanut shells off the main floor, stopping occasionally to pluck a penny or a nickel from the sticky mass, wipe it on his shirt sleeve and thrust it into the pocket of his overalls.

Liam, the Silver Dollar's owner was behind the bar wiping it down with a rag."Damn, Liam," said Durken. "Every time I walk in here, you're wiping down that bar. I'm surprised you ain't worn a hole through it by now."

"You know what they say, Durken: Cleanliness is next to godliness. I heard you got gored pretty good."

"Yep. I'm here strictly for medicinal purposes."

Liam turned to McAfee. "And what's your excuse this early in the morning, boyo?"

"Preventive medicine."

Liam held the whiskey bottle up and studied it. "I'm a red-haired son or Erin. I don't need an excuse." They all had a laugh at that, and McAfee put a five dollar gold piece on the bar and said, "Pour yourself one while you're at it."

Liam poured three shots and raised his in the air. "To your speedy recovery, Durken."

As they knocked back their shots, a stocky man in trail dusty clothes came through the swinging doors. He looked around the dim room, his eyes getting used to the light. "Hello, my friend," said Liam. What can I get for you?"

"Just some information. My name's Jake Ketchum." He could have been thirty, forty, or fifty under that tough shell of trail grit, wind scrub, and sunburn that all cowboys cultivate from hard years in the saddle. He had a permanent crease across his forehead that looked like a frown wrinkle, but up close McAfee recognized as a knife scar.

"I'm looking for two cowboys, friends of mine, Hank Martin and Ed Durst. Hank's my brother-in-law. They were supposed to go with me on a drive from Denver two weeks ago and never showed up. They sent a telegram when they left Kansas, and they planned on coming through here on their way."

"Can't say I've heard the names. What do these fellows look like?" said McAfee.

"Ed Durst is nothing special. A little shorter than you two, bald on top. He has a fringe of red hair and a big red nose, and he's a little wall-eyed. Hank's tall with wide shoulders and a thick moustache."

"That sounds like half of Nevada," said Liam, " and that's just the women."

Everyone laughed but Ketchum. His mouth pressed into a taut line. "I like a joke same's any man, boys, but this ain't funny. My wife's half crazy worrying about her little brother, and if I don't find him, I don't know how she'll turn out."

"Did they maybe run out of money and hire on with somebody along the way? I'm McAfee, and this is Durken. We're foremen at the Triple Six. I know we haven't hired anybody new lately. Nobody came asking, either."

"That's something I'll have to look into."

"You talk with Harvey Bennet, the sheriff?"

Ketchum nodded. "He said he hadn't heard anything one way or the other."

Liam poured a shot and slid the glass across the bar to Ketchum. "You must be dry, Mister Ketchum. Have one on the house."

"Thank you, but no. I gave up drink five years ago. It was that or lose my wife."

"Well, sir," said Durken, "For a man to do that and what you're doing now, she must be an exceptional woman. You have our compliments. If you don't mind my asking, where'd you get that forehead?"

Ketchum drew a finger from one end of the crease to the other. "A bayonet at Gettysburg."

"McAfee and I were scouts in the March to the Sea. I won't ask you which army, Jake. Way I see it, now it's over and we're all on the same side again."

McAfee added, "If you come back this way, look us up. we'll keep our ears open. And I would feel better knowing you found your friends. Good luck to you."

Ketchum nodded curtly. "Thank you, men." He turned on his heel and walked out.

Durken gazed through the swinging doors. "That's what happens when you break the urn."

VII

The General's private car, still hitched to an engine and coal tender stood on a rail siding a few miles outside town. As he pulled up to the car in the buckboard, Durken remarked, "Same old rolling whorehouse."

As a tormenting joke, when Sherman requested a private rail car to travel through the Territories, the War Department requisitioned the colorful private car that disgraced Secretary of War William Bellknap used to travel with his mistresses and concubines before his sins caught up with him. The gaudy green and yellow car looked like a cross between a gypsy wagon and Cleopatra's barge, and Sherman, accustomed to sleeping in a fly tent the same as his men on the battlefield ground his teeth every time he set foot in it.

A pair of privates at order arms flanked the iron steps onto the platform. As they climbed down from the buckboard, McAfee said, "Durken and McAfee here reporting to General Sherman."

One of the soldiers said. "Please wait here a moment," and stepped onto the platform. He rapped on the door, spoke to someone inside, and stepped back holding the door open. "Please come up, gentlemen."

As they climbed the steps, McAfee said, "Do you see horses that might belong to Tate and his man?"

"Nope." Durken was taking one step at a time, using his hands on the rail as much as his good leg to climb. It was slow going, but McAfee knew better than to offer him any help.

"Inside please," the private said. The cowboys stepped into the car and found the General behind the French Provincial table he used as a desk, looking as if he'd never left the chair. He pulled his cigar from the corner of his mouth and said, "Durken, what the devil did you do to yourself this time?"

Durken grinned. "Got gored by a buffalo, General."

"That's the trouble with us old war horses. We don't know when to quit, and we probably wouldn't if we did." He looked McAfee up and down. "At least you're whole. Oh well, half a loaf and all that." He indicated a heavy wooden bench in front of the table. "Sit down."

"What happened to the fancy chairs that were in here last time?"

"They weren't designed for prolonged use by military rumps. They fell apart pretty fast. I'm riding one of the last two."

"How's Captain Harper?" said McAfee. Harper was a casualty of the fighting with the Cat Warriors.

"He's pensioned out at my request. He didn't lose his leg, but he can't walk without a cane. He went back to the family farm in Indiana. Last I heard he was breeding quarter horses."

Durken said, "I'm glad he pulled through. He's a good man and a good officer." McAfee nodded in agreement.

"He'd've been dead for sure if it hadn't been for the two of you." Sherman struck a match and relit his cigar, wreathing his unshaven face in smoke.

"And we'd've likely been dead if it weren't for him," said McAfee. "That's what fighting back to back's all about."

Sherman rolled his cigar between his thumb and forefinger, studying the ash at the tip. "I hate to do this to you, but I need your help with a classified situation. I trust you two with my life, but the almighty War Department doesn't trust anybody. Raise your right hands." In ninety seconds, McAfee and Durken were once again in the U. S. Army, but this time they were lieutenants.

"Ever hear of the Patapa? The Snake Clan?"

"Heard of them," said Durken, "but I thought they were just a legend, a story the squaws used to scare their children into line."

"Not exactly," said McAfee. "I think they were a going concern around the turn of the century in the Dakotas, but the other tribes joined forces to hunt them down and wipe them out. As I recall, they stole children and sacrificed them to their god."

"Goddess," said Sherman. "Ki-no Na-te, the Snake Mother." He pulled a black and white tintype from the pile of papers on his desk. "This picture was taken ten days ago across the border in Utah. The nearest town is Casselman." He set the picture on the desk and handed a magnifier to McAfee.

The stark image showed a Conestoga wagon. The horses were slumped in their traces. A man in overalls and a work coat lay face up on the ground clutching a rifle, his face a blackened mask with bulging eyes and a protruding tongue. A woman in a calico dress sprawled across the seat of the wagon, her head tilted back over its edge, her mouth wide in a silent scream. Like the man's, her flesh was unnaturally darkened like a face in a minstrel show. Her eyes bulged like boiled eggs.

"Family Bible and other papers in the wagon identified these folks as Reynald and Maria Posset from Minnesota."

"Any idea what killed them, General?"

"Snakes." He tapped the picture with the tip of his finger. "Both of them full of venom from at least a dozen snake bites each; the horses too."

"I never heard of a rattlesnake bite killing a horse. I always thought they were too big. A rattler doesn't have that much venom."

"That should give you an idea of how many snakes there were. And that's not the worst." Sherman turned his face away from the ghastly picture. "There was a child with them, a little girl. Her name is Eloise, and she can't be found."

"Any other casualties?" Durken said, "He's got his rifle in hand."

"Never fired," said Sherman. "That's one of the mysteries. However this happened, it happened fast, and it happened in broad daylight."

"Maybe one of the horses stepped in a nest of rattlers. I've seen some with as many as fifty snakes in them. Disturbing a rattler nest is like kicking an anthill."

"They weren't on an established trail. The men who took that picture didn't find any trace of a nest; the ground there's hard as iron. What worries me most is the girl. Rattlesnakes don't kidnap children."

Durken nodded. "That's so, but maybe she escaped and ran away."

"If she did, nobody's found her yet."

"How can we help, General?" McAfee said, staring at the picture.

"Try to pick up a trail and maybe find the girl. And if some tribe or cult's responsible, find the sons-of-bitches that did this and stop them before they do it again."

"General, it's been ten days. I figure the trail is cold by now."

"That's true, but if you see the place, you might find things in common the next time it happens."

"You think there'll be a next time?"

He stubbed out his cigar. "If the Patapa are back, I'm afraid so. If the newspapers get hold of this business, it'll cause a panic. Washington's trying to paint a picture of safe passage west to promote settlers, and a story like this would scare them all back to Plymouth Rock. We've had the Indian situation under control for the most part since we put down Red Hawk's uprising, but something like this could set a backlash in motion that could start the Indian wars all over again."

"What troops are in the area?" Durken said, frowning at the picture.

"Colonel named Stuyvesant's got a battalion of around six hundred men in that sector in Utah, and there's been no Indian trouble there since the Bear River massacre all but wiped out the Shoshoni in '63. I hate to think trouble's starting all over again."

"What about Tate and Black? Why's the Secret Service interested in this situation?"

"Your guess is as good as mine. I don't see what this incident has to do with national security, but here they are. I admit that Tate's as good as any as far as investigation goes, but he doesn't have your savvy when it comes to tracking, nor your knowledge of Indians or of the territory. I need your eyes."

"We can go look at the place where this happened, but I won't be able to ride for another week," Durken said.

"McAfee could go now, and you could join him in a couple of days."

McAfee nodded. "I suppose we could work it that way." He turned to Durken. "In the meantime, you could pay Seven Stars a visit and see what he knows about Ki-no Na-te and the Patapa."

Durken nodded agreement, but McAfee could see by his face that he didn't like the idea. "Anybody else riding with him?"

"Tate and Black are headed to Casselman now, and a handful of soldiers from the outpost at Silver Forks are already on hand."

"I was a little bit surprised to see Tate running your errands today."

"That was intentional. I was being a bastard, just letting him know that I'm in charge here, and it did my heart good to make him play fetch. Made him acknowledge my command." He eyed Durken over the end of his cigar. "I know there's bad blood between you two and Tate. I don't like him either, but Washington insisted he be a part of this. He's a cog in the works. Try to not kill him."

"Only if we have to, General," Durken said, with no trace of irony. "But it will be an effort."

VIII

Outside, McAfee took his gear from the buckboard. "Did you mean it'd be an effort to not kill Tate, or an effort to try to not kill him?"

"Maybe a little of both."

"I'll do my best to get along with Tate for the General's sake, but I can't make any promises either."

"That paper the General gave you says Tate and his men have to take orders from us, right?"

"'In the field' were the General's words. He rides with me; he does what I tell him."

Durken grinned. "I'm almost sorry I can't come along. I'd have the shiniest boots in Nevada."

Casselman, the town where the wagon was found would be a good two days' ride for McAfee. "With a little luck, I'll make Portman before dark," he said. "As I recall the hotel there doesn't have more cockroaches than flies. I can at least sleep in a bed."

"You're getting soft," Durken said with a snort. "Too many nights in the bunkhouse."

"Naah. I spent about as much time sleeping on the ground as I have on a tick the last ten years, and I've developed an appreciation for the merits of both."

"There's no time now, but you'll have to fill me in on the merits of sleeping on the ground sometime. I missed that lesson somewhere along the way."

"It's pretty simple. You roll over, there's nowhere to fall." McAfee cinched the girth on Sweetheart's saddle. "You will give my regards to Sarah, won't you?"

"She won't be happy."

"I expect not, but just tell her I'll be back."

"If I had my choice, I'd be riding for Casselman, and you'd be driving the buckboard back to the Triple Six, either that or we'd both be riding off together."

"Some decisions are made for us, Durken."

"Yep." He climbed onto the seat of the buckboard. "Don't make it taste any better."

Durken flicked the reins and the wagon rolled one way as McAfee and Sweetheart rode the other.

It was mid-afternoon when Durken drove the buckboard through the gate of the Triple Six. The crew was still out with the herd as he climbed down to unhitch the horses. He looked back at the house and saw the curtains move in the same upstairs window McAfee had seen earlier. He figured he wouldn't have to give Miss Sarah the news; she knew it already.

Sam Tatty, the hand Eldridge liked to call his "groom" came in from the other end of the stable as Durken was currying the horses with a stiff straw brush. Sam was tall and broad-shouldered with a thick shock of white hair that belied his strength. He could manage any horse, no matter how wild, but he preferred to win the animal over rather than imposing his will by sheer force.

"You take good care of the beasts, Durken. Not everybody does."

"I figure they work as hard as I do. Besides, the way I see it, it's kinda like sharpening my knife." He put a hand on the pommel of the twelve-inch Bowie at his belt. "When you need it's no time to take a half hour out for maintenance."

"How's your leg?"

"Still hurts like hell if I lean on it the wrong way. Too bad you can't tend it. The way you have with healing the animals, I'd be jumping fences already."

Sam looked over Durken's shoulder. "Here comes Maggie."

Durken turned his head and saw the cook striding across the yard, fists clenched, her apron dancing in the breeze. He turned to say something to Sam, but Sam had made a discreet exit.

"So ye're back, Durken." She stood arms akimbo. "And your partner in mischief?"

"On his way to Casselman for the General, and that's as much as I can tell you."

"And you?"

"Here I am." Durken put his hands out, palms up is an open gesture reminiscent of statues of the Savior.

"But for how long?"

"Maggie, I can't ride with this leg, and I sure as hell can't chase Indians or outlaws in a buckboard."

"But as soon as you can throw that leg over a saddle, you'll be off right after McAfee. That poor girl is crying her eyes out right now. When she saw you come back without him, it about broke her heart."

"Maggie, he's just doing some scouting for the General, that's all. You know, we always come back."

"Aye," she said, her eyes blazing, "but every time you do, there's a little piece missing here or there, and it ain't all bones and flesh, and someday, there won't be enough of you left to come back, or enough of you to want to." She threw up her hands. "I may as well talk to that horse as to you, Durken. I can't be mad with you any more than I can with a dog that steals a steak off the table when my back's turned. It's just his nature and yours too, I'd venture to say, but that don't make it easy to abide."

Before Durken could think of a response, Maggie turned and strode out of the stable the way she had come. She turned back, just past the door. "Oh, and Himself wants to speak to you as soon as you're done with the horses."

Durken took his time putting away the tack and throwing some hay in Thunder's stall, even though Sam offered to do it for him. That done, he heaved a sigh of resignation and limped across the yard to the Mansion, where Eldridge was waiting to pepper his ears.

Eldridge sat, as he usually did, in the banker's chair behind his desk like a king on his throne or maybe a feudal baron in his castle. Durken did his best to disguise his limp, but it was no use.

"So, Durken, what task did his majesty Sherman put you on this time?"

Durken tipped his hat back but didn't take it off. "If you don't mind, could I sit down? My leg's not quite up to supporting me yet."

"Sure. Be my guest. Sit. It's what you've been doing for more than a week, anyway."

Durken held his tongue, although his injured leg was largely Eldridge's fault. Eldridge could read the smoldering anger in his eyes at the insult, and changed his tack. "You came back, but McAfee didn't. What's going on?"

"First, with all due respect, Mister Eldridge, I'm not able to tell you what's going on. The word the General used is 'classified.'"

"I figured as much," Eldridge snorted. "That son of a bitch would make it a classified mission if he sent you across the street to buy him cigars."

"I can tell you it's nothing so trivial."

"And what about McAfee? How long will he be gone? Or is that classified, too?"

"That I can't say, either. He can ride, and I can't. He rode off and I didn't. He could be back in a few days, or a week, or a month. No telling."

"Well that's just wonderful. In the meantime, with him gone and you disabled, I have to run the Triple Six with the leftovers." He took a cigar from the humidor on his desk and snipped it with a silver cutter.

"In all fairness, Harley Wilcox is an able man. He knows his work, and he's been here long enough to have the lay of the land. I'd say he has it all under control."

Eldridge took his time lighting his cigar. He pointed the glowing end at Durken. "If that's so, then maybe I should just put him in charge and you two can go roam free wherever the General points his finger."

"That would be your decision, Mister Eldridge. I can speak only for myself, but I knew how to walk, breathe, and shit before I ever saw this place, and I figure I wouldn't forget how somewhere else. And by the way, if Wilcox does foreman's work, you oughta give him foreman's pay."

Eldridge's face reddened all the way to back of his scalp at Durken's casual dismissal of the threat.

"Now, as for me, I expect I'll be called to join McAfee as soon as I'm able, unless, of course, he comes back here in the meantime. If that should happen, I'll make sure that you know as soon as I do. Now, if you'll excuse me, I'm going back to the bunkhouse to have Charlie put a fresh poultice on my leg to quick up my recovery so's I can get back to real work." Durken stood and walked out of Eldridge's study. He left the door open to match Eldridge's gaping mouth.

Durken passed through the kitchen on his way out and found Maggie scrubbing out a kettle. "So, what do you think, Maggie? Did I talk myself out of a job?"

She looked up and her brow furrowed. "And how should I know?"

"I figured you were listening at the door the whole time. I'd say you just started scrubbing that pot. You haven't even rolled up your sleeves."

"Oh!" she snorted. She wagged a finger at him. "Sometimes you're too smart for your own good, Durken."

"Kept me alive this long." He put two fingers to the brim of his hat. "Goodnight, Maggie."

The walk back to the bunkhouse seemed a little bit shorter every time as his leg healed, but it was still a torment. He almost wished he hadn't ruined the buffalo's head so that every time he went into Eldridge's study he could stare into its glass eyes and say, "I won; you lost."

Supper was about over, and Charlie had to scrape the pots to dish up a whole plate of pork and beans for Durken. As he ate, Wilcox came over and pulled up a chair. He straddled it with his arms over the chair back. "So, what hornet flew up Eldridge's pant leg today?"

"Looks as if you'll be in charge for a while. McAfee's going to be away, and I can't ride. I told Eldridge you were he man for the job. Do a good job, and maybe you'll be in charge permanent."

"I don't know I'd want that," said Wilcox. "You and McAfee temper his steel pretty good; otherwise, half the hands would've quit a long time ago. I'm not sure I can do the same."

"Time'll tell, Harley. Time'll tell."

Charlie came in from the kitchen lean-to. "We change your dressing now, Durken."

Durken rose slowly from his chair. "Okay, Charlie. Let's do 'er."

Durken followed Charlie back into the kitchen and undid his suspenders. He shucked off his dungarees and boots and lay on Charlie's bunk beside the stove. Charlie held a lamp in one hand and pulled open the slit in Durken's union suit exposing the bandage over his injury. He peeled away the bandage and Durken grimaced as it stuck to the healing skin.

Charlie brought the lamp closer. He squinted at the raw patch of flesh. "It is swollen, more than yesterday. It has to be drained."

"What are you gonna do? Cut it open?"

Charlie shook his head. "A new cut could bring new infection. I will do something I learned as a boy."

Charlie busied himself at the stove for a few moments and came back to the cot holding a glass bowl a little larger than a billiard ball. "This will smart some, but it has to be hot." He pressed the edges of the bowl into Durken's skin surrounding the wound and held it in place.

Durken sucked in a sharp breath. "What's going on, Charlie?"

"You watch, you see."

As the glass cooled, and the air inside it, a vacuum formed, drawing at the wound. The skin bulged into the cup, and Durken saw small beads of yellow began to ooze around the stitches. In a few moments, the swelling was gone, the infection drawn out.

Charlie took away the bowl and gently wiped away the pus. "Maybe now you heal faster."

"That's some trick, Charlie. I never heard of anything like that."

"You live long enough; you learn enough to live longer." He folded some crushed roots and herbs into a clean piece of linen and pressed it onto the wound. He tied it in place with a strip of tow sack and nodded his head in satisfaction.

Durken stood gingerly. "I'll be damned. It don't hurt as much now as it did when I came in here."

"Tomorrow, we see what comes of it."

"Here's hoping. It can't heal too fast for me."

IX

McAfee lay on the bed, eyes wide open, though he could see nothing in the pitch dark room of the Portman Hotel. It seemed that the cockroach population had overtaken the flies and they all seemed to be having a festival in his room. He fumbled for his trousers and dug the box of matches from his pocket, cursing as something with spindly legs ran over the back of his hand.

The match flared and dark shapes scattered to darker corners and gaps in the baseboard. He lit the candle sitting on a small stand beside the bed and rolled onto his back. He closed his eyes and hoped it wouldn't burn down the hotel before he woke up.

It had taken him until sunset to reach Portman, and the telegraph office was closed. He'd have to wait for the morning to see whether there was further word from the General or from Tate.

Tate. McAfee hated to be pushed together with him again, but as the General said, "orders are orders." He hoped that Tate had learned a few things from their last mission together, if you could call his working at cross purposes to them "together." But based on his encounter with Durken, McAfee figured his attitude was pretty much the same.

In some ways, it was a compliment that the General called on him and Durken when a problem couldn't be solved by the Book, the Army Field Manual, but at the same time being drawn into the murky political cesspool of the Secret Service made it a curse. The Service's goals and aims often drifted far afield of its stated mission to "protect the National interest." They had wanted to learn the secrets of the Cat Warriors and use them to field an invincible army of monstrosities against any perceived enemy, foreign or home grown. To McAfee, the Secret Service was every bit as evil as the forces they fought, and every bit as worthy of opposition.

Just like the cockroaches, McAfee thought. Shine a light on them and they scatter and hide because people wouldn't abide what they do in the dark. His last thoughts were of Sarah as he drifted into a dreamless sleep.

X

McAfee woke to a knock at his door. He rose from the bed and as a precaution born of habit, drew his pistol from its holster and stood to the side of the door before he spoke. "Yeah?"

A wheezy voice he recognized as the scrawny desk clerk's said, "Telegram for you, Mister McAfee."

"Slide it under the door."

The corner of a folded piece of paper poked into sight. "Shall I wait for a reply?"

McAfee put a toe on the telegram and pulled it into the room, knowing better than to crouch to pick it up and make an easy target through the lower half of the door. "No need to wait." He dropped a fifty-cent piece on the floor and nudged it into the hallway.

"Thank you kindly, sir."

McAfee unfolded the paper. The message was military simple: "RENDEZVOUS CASSELMAN SERGEANT CULLISON STOP. It was signed simply, TATE.

McAfee pulled on his trousers and boots, and as he buttoned his shirt, he thought about breakfast, the long ride ahead, and Sarah, though not in that order.

XI

After two helpings of Charlie's bacon and eggs, Durken headed for the barn and the buckboard. The Monatai village was a good two hour's ride on horseback and would take even longer by wagon. There he would find the blind chief Seven Stars.

Educated by Jesuit missionaries as a boy and groomed for the Catholic priesthood, Seven Stars was fluent in a number of languages and as an adolescent became the personal secretary of Father Leonardo, a former Vatican expert on ancient civilizations and pagan religions. As the priest's sight failed him, Seven Stars read to him from the forbidden sacred books of his research and learned terrible secrets of gods and monsters before the Jesuit's death ended their relationship.

Now blind himself, Seven Stars remained chief of the Monatai tribe and was a comrade in arms to Durken and McAfee in the protection of his people from evils human and otherworldly.

Durken approached the high mesa from the south; the village was tucked behind it, shielded from the scouring dust storms and blazing afternoon sun. He pulled back the reins at the foot of the mesa, halting the buckboard, raised both hands palms open, and waited. In a moment, a brave with a rifle appeared at the top of the mesa.

"Friend Durken," called down the brave.

"Black Feather," Durken replied. "I come to see your chief."

"Enter as a friend."

Durken twitched the reins and the buckboard rattled around the mesa and into the protected hollow where he saw the ranks of tipis and the great communal lodge. The tribe had grown in the last year, prospering with good seasons of hunting and agriculture, yet they still maintained a watchful vigilance, knowing that at any time, the peaceful days could end.

Seven Stars was a chief who advocated peace with the U.S. government, but was a thorn in its side because of his education. Driven from the Church, Seven Stars turned his intellect and his study to matters of law, and now fought his battles in court, winning concessions and protecting the conditions of treaties to the exasperation of politicians and soldiers alike.

A young brave took the reins of the horses, and Durken climbed from the seat of the wagon to the ground. He nodded respectfully to the brave and followed as another led him through the village. In a moment, he stood outside a conical tipi whose lodge poles were covered with animal hides, which were in turn decorated with native symbols. In a few places, Durken saw lines of script, some in a language he recognized as Latin, and a few in languages he'd never seen elsewhere.

"Durken, my friend, you come alone." The voice from inside the tipi was deep and resonant, its English spoken with the élan of a Shakespearean actor. The flap parted and Seven Stars strode out. The chief was a regal presence, a Greek statue in buckskin who forewent traditional braiding and wore his shoulder-length hair loose and free. All that marred his handsome visage was a band of rough weave tapestry across his blind eyes.

"Howdy, Seven Stars," Durken said, coming closer.

Seven Stars cocked his head toward the sound."Your step is less than confident," the Chief said. "You have been hurt."

"Gored by a buffalo," Durken said.

"And the buffalo?"

"The tribe had grown in the last year..."

"In my belly."

Seven Stars laughed. "Then our shaggy friend got the worst of the encounter." He paused. "And where is McAfee?"

"He's on his way to Casselman in the Utah territory on a mission for the General. That's why I'm here too."

Seven Stars' smile faded. There was no love lost between him and Sherman, whom he saw as the guiding hand of enforcement and intimidation. "Ah yes, the sainted General. He who would keep the peace by waging war. What is it that you seek from me?"

"I need to know what you can tell me about the Patapa and Ki-no Na-te."

Seven Stars' face hardened. He gestured toward the tent, "This is not for all ears. Please come inside and sit with me."

Durken followed Seven Stars into the tipi and sat on a mound of buffalo robes as the Chief closed the flap. "Those are names I have not heard in a long time. Why are they spoken now?"

"Chief, there has been an incident." Durken went on to describe the deaths of the Possets and the disappearance of their daughter.

"And this is the only one?"

"The only one we know of. Maybe it was just a fluke and they ran into a nest of rattlers, and maybe the girl ran off, and died elsewhere, or somebody found her and took her in, but the General isn't willing to take a chance on it, especially after the Cat Warrior uprising."

Seven Stars was silent for a moment. He turned his face toward Durken, and Durken felt as if the Chief's blind eyes saw him through the tapestry band and looked into his head, his heart, and his soul. "I do not trust the motives of the Great Sherman, nor do I trust those of his masters, but I know your heart, and that of McAfee. If the Patapa have returned, they are a threat to all people, and I will tell you what I know."

Seven Stars rose and from a beaded bag, he took a small pouch. He sprinkled some of the contents over the fire in the middle of the tent, and a cloud of reddish, sweet-smelling smoke wafted upward. Seven Stars spoke words in his tribal tongue, and he sat again, cross-legged, taking a deep breath of the fumes.

"Take a breath, Durken, to shield you from evil spirits as we discuss their secrets."

Durken hesitated a few seconds, then breathed deep. The inside of the tipi darkened, and the smoke seemed to probe every crevice of his being. His head felt a trifle light, then the chamber brightened, and Seven Stars began to speak.

XII

"**F**or each thing in creation, there is an origin, and for each tribe, there is a story of that origin, but the world around, serpents are held in suspicion and fear. The Bible calls the Devil "the original serpent," and has thus branded the snake wherever he may be found, and in whatever form, an enemy, an idea spread among the Tribes by missionaries. Most tribes agreed, and likewise see the snake as a destroyer, but a few revered the snake as a protector.

"The Patapa of the Northern Plains were one such. Their legends tell of a warm spring in the first times when their people were weak and starving after a hard winter. But instead of relief and comfort, the new season brought new peril. The wolves, hundreds of them, driven southward by the severe cold and lack of game, surrounded their village. For a time, the Patapa ringed their village with fires to hold the wolves at bay, but they soon had burned all but the last of their wood.

"The wolves circled the village and once the sun set, began closing their circle. The moon rose, and the leader of the wolf pack, a great grey beast reared his head and howled. The pack answered, the wolves began their attack, and the Patapa were sure that their end had come.

"Then the ground shook and a bluff behind the village opened up, and from the bowels of the earth poured a torrent of snakes, their rattles whirring, and their fangs dripping venom. And from their midst rose a towering figure, a woman but not a woman, Ki-no Na-Te. She had the torso of a woman, and a woman's beautiful face, but her arms and breasts were covered in scales, and where hair would be a woman's crown of glory, a mass of snakes writhed and hissed.

"In a voice like a windstorm, she said, 'I am Ki-no Na-Te, the Snake Mother. Pledge yourselves to me, and I will deliver you from death.' And in their desperation the Patapa elders cried, 'Yes, Snake Mother, save us, and we will do as you say.'

"Ki-no Na- Te raised her arms and the snakes surged forth like oil poured on water, in a spreading circle to meet the closing one of the wolves. The Snake Mother seized the wolf pack leader by the scruff of his neck, and bit through his throat like a bear trap. The battle was terrible, and in the end, no wolf stood. And the Patapa bowed to Ki-no- Na-Te and said, 'You have delivered us from death. We will worship and obey you.'

"Ki-no Na- Te said, 'I am tired and hungry from the fight. Give me a child that I may eat and restore myself.' She seized an infant from his mother's arms and held the screaming child aloft. Her jaw swung as wide as a stile, and she crammed the child into her maw.

"And the terrified elders said, 'Goddess, so many of our children died of hunger this winter that we have almost none, and if we give them all to you, our tribe will die out within a generation, having no one to carry on.'

"And Ki-no- Na-te said, 'I see the sense in your words. Do not sacrifice your children. Instead, seek out a child elsewhere every moon and bring it to me that I may be fed and be satisfied, and I will be your protector and benefactor. Fail me, and die.'

"And so the Patapa ranged far and wide in that terrible season, stealing children to sacrifice to their goddess. The child's tribe would mount an attack, and they would fall to the snakes that protected the Patapa village. Soon, the other tribes met in council and decided that this must end. They formed an alliance and resolved as one, to wage war on the Patapa."

"Well," Durken interrupted, "Couldn't the Snake Mother just set the rattlers on the other tribes? I expect that battle wouldn't last too long."

"That would have been so, were it not for the wisdom of a Cherokee chief named Red Cub. He rose in the Council of the Chiefs and said, 'Let us not attack at once, but instead, after the harvest, let us mass our force and attack on the first frost when the snakes are slow and sleepy.' The others saw the wisdom of the plan and agreed that it would be done.

"The shamans of the tribes wove a magic lariat of the webs of spiders to capture and contain the snake goddess in its sticky loops and they set out in the cold sunset. Red Cub led the charge on the village, and when the Patapa cried to their goddess for help, the bluff opened and the snakes poured out like a river to repel the attackers, but unlike the warmth of their den, they found numbing cold and frost. The sluggish serpents were easy prey for the tomahawks and knives of the braves.

"And when Ki-no Na-Te came shrieking from her lair, the shamans threw the lariat over her. The more she writhed and thrashed, the more tightly she became wound in the sticky strands, until she could no longer move. And the shamans tied her to horses and dragged her to the edge of the world and with a great heave, threw her over. The Patapa were put to death, every one of them, and that was the end of it."

"And she never came back?"

"According to the legend, she has never come back to this land, but snake women have appeared in stories from other parts of the Earth. Of course, the problem with myths is that they have no distinct time in their telling. She could have appeared long before she did here or long after. My Hopi brothers still honor her banishment in a ceremonial dance they perform with live rattlesnakes."

Neither spoke for a time. Finally Durken broke the silence. "Why didn't they kill her when they had the chance?"

"In a sense they did, depriving her of her faithful followers. Without worshippers, does a god remain a god?"

"Then why not just kill her and be done with it?"

"My friend," said Seven Stars, "has McAfee ever talked about Manachaeism?"

"Can't say as he has. What's it mean?"

"It is a philosophy that includes, put simply, that evil must exist so that good might have purpose. Father Leonardo and Father Giocamo debated it often. It is anathema to the Christian belief that the Second Coming of Christ will bring evil's end. The religions of the Tribes embrace the oneness of the world, and the need to maintain its balance; thus, the belief that evil cannot be destroyed, only confined. To destroy Ki-no Na-Te would be to upset that balance."

"Kinda like keeping the natural order of things."

"Yes. The evil is put aside, but good must always be on the watch to see that it does not return. Given the right circumstance and knowledge, Ki-No Na-Te could always be summoned from beyond. And Durken,"

"Yes, Seven Stars?"

"There is one other piece of wisdom for you to consider. It is said that you should avoid killing a snake, especially a rattlesnake. To kill one means that you will soon see others; and should you kill another, many will surround you until you can no longer find a way out."

"I'll keep that in mind."

XIII

Casselman was slightly less a town than Bacon Rock, likely because it didn't have the benefit of railroad tracks. It was a little cattle drive way station at the end of one of the roads that branched out like fingers from some county seat a few days' ride away. A single street ran the length of Casselman, like a dusty furrow ploughed between rows of wooden buildings. A few stores, a few houses, but missing a few signs of civilization; no bank, not even a hotel, a church, or a jail.

But at the far end of the street stood a building with a covered porch across its front and a balcony overhead populated by a few gaudily painted dance hall floozies. The weathered sign across the front of the building said only Saloon. Figures, thought McAfee. The vices arrive before the virtues out here. The jail'll get here someday, and so will the church, but in the meantime, life's pretty much what you might expect. It's no wonder that family kept moving on.

McAfee tied Sweetheart to the rail outside the saloon. From above came a few coos and whistles from the women. He looked up, touched the brim of his hat and said, "Ladies," then crossed the porch to the swinging doors. Inside, the saloon was pretty much like most; a long bar spanned the back of the room with ranks of bottles and glasses on display behind it. A dozen or so round tables filled the floor space and in one corner, a piano sat silent. The other corner was dominated by a staircase that led to a railed walkway with doors opening onto it, presumably quarters for the women.

At a table in a darker corner of the room, a man in a dusty Cavalry uniform with sergeant's chevrons sat with a near empty bottle of whiskey. Beside him a stocky man in wire-rimmed glasses sat smoking a corn cob pipe. When McAfee looked a little closer, he saw that the pipe was packed with the stub of a cigar.

The smoker was dressed in a suit coat over a flowered vest and a stock like the ones Eldridge favored, though a little shabby and worn by comparison, and tan trousers tucked into knee high black boots. McAfee strolled over to the table and said to the sergeant, "You Cullison?" He nodded. "I'm McAfee."

Cullison kicked out a chair and said, "Have a seat. I'm Jim Cullison, and this fella's Titus Willoughby." Willoughby nodded and said "Hullo," around the stem of his pipe.

"You supposed to take me to meet Tate?" McAfee said.

Cullison nodded again. "Soon's I finish this bottle. Maybe you'd like to help."

"Don't mind if I do," McAfee said, pouring himself a shot, quickly understanding why the sergeant came himself on a fetch duty instead of sending a private.

Cullison was the kind of man who made a horse look like a pony. He was over six-six and had shoulders like an ox yoke. His iron grey hair merged with mutton chop sideburns and a thick moustache that all but hid his upper lip. Broken veins across his fleshy nose and cheeks testified to a life of hard drinking by a man who had gotten as far in life as he ever would but didn't seem to mind.

Willoughby poured one for himself and another for Cullison. "What's your role in this business, Mister McAfee?"

McAfee eyed him carefully. "I'd say you first, Willoughby." He looked to Cullison.

Cullison made an offhand gesture. "He's on the mission. Tate sent for him. Go ahead, Willoughby, give him your pedigree." Cullison pronounced the last word with emphasis on the long-voweled syllable.

"Kentucky?" said McAfee.

Cullison looked startled. "How'd you know?"

"The way you say your words. I knew a few of the Bluegrass boys in the war. I'm guessing you changed uniforms after Appomattox."

"No, sir. I fought for the Union right down the line. Joined up before the insurrection. Some of the fellows felt obligated to go back home, but I knew what side of my bread had the molasses."

"And you, Willoughby?"

"I am a resident of the world, my friend. Titus Willoughby, the Snake Master, late of the Doctor Magnus Traveling Medicine Show. I was invited here by Agent Tate to look into what he calls an 'unusual situation.'" He puffed at his pipe and the end of the cigar glowed like a railroad lantern. "I arrived here a scant hour before you did."

McAfee knocked back his drink. "I was sent here by General Sherman for the same purpose."

Willoughby leaned forward as if anticipating more, but Cullison spoke up. "Sherman, eh? I've been out here chasing redskins for him since the war was over, but I've never seen hide nor hair of the man. I guess he has lots of papers to push."

McAfee poured another shot. "You'd think different if you rode with him. I scouted for him in the Georgia campaign. He hasn't changed. He has his hands full, same as you do, maybe more so, just with different things. By the way, is the local sheriff involved in this operation?"

The sergeant shook his head. "Sheriff Curtis Parker works three counties, and from what I hear from the locals, he only shows up around here at election time. He's about as useful as a tit on a turkey."

Cullison eyed the last inch of the whiskey in the bottle. He tipped his head back and put it to his lips. His Adam's apple bobbed as he gulped down the last swallow. He grabbed a handful of his slouch hat, slapped it on his head and said, "Let's ride."

Cullison and Willoughby headed down the street to the livery for their horses while McAfee climbed aboard Sweetheart. Above him, the girls were tittering over some joke. One of them called down to him, but he ignored her and clucked his tongue at Sweetheart, who set off down the street.

McAfee considered his new companions. He'd known plenty of men like Cullison, people who couldn't control their own lives and let the Army do it for them. Most of them ended up the same in time, piss-mean and ruthless when given an order. They advanced in rank as far as sergeant, and the Army kept them there, useful where they were. Willoughby was a mystery. Why did Tate invite a circus act to the party? "I guess I'll find out soon enough," said McAfee, and he rode toward the horsemen waiting at the edge of town.

XIV

s he drove the buckboard back to the Triple Six, Durken pondered Seven Stars' words. He'd killed many rattlers in his day, but never one that came back double. He shrugged it off as a tribal legend, and set his thoughts to supper and a good slug of whiskey to dull the aching in his leg.

When he drove the wagon through the gateway to the ranch, Durken could see Harley Wilcox coming around the back of the Mansion, likely leaving a lecture from Eldridge. Like most of the ranch hands, Harley was relegated to the back door of the house instead of the front. He saw Durken on the buckboard and crossed the yard to meet him.

"You're foreman now," said Durken with a chuckle. "Seems to me you ought to be coming and going through the front."

"While it lasts," said Wilcox. "About the time I get used to it, you and McAfee'll be in charge again, and I'll forget myself and go through the wrong door and end up with my hide tanned and stretched on the wall of his trophy room."

"I guess he didn't blister you like he does me or McAfee, I see your ears are still holding up your hat."

"He gave me enough," said Wilcox. "I don't know how you can stand it, being accountable for every little thing that happens here."

"You were never in the Army. McAfee and I had to put up with a slew of sergeants. When it comes to dressing down somebody, by comparison Eldridge is an amateur. By the way, any word yet from McAfee?"

Wilcox shook his head. "Nope."

"Then I'll see you at supper. These horses ain't gonna put themselves away."

Wilcox nodded and turned for the bunkhouse. Durken twitched the reins and the horses plodded across the yard toward the hay and water of the stable.

As he hung up their tack, Maggie walked through the cross-buck doors. "So ye're back," she said, standing like a sturdy oak growing out of the straw that covered the earthen floor. Durken felt a twinge of irritation at her repeated tactic of cornering him while he was in the middle of a task he had to finish and couldn't escape.

"Happy to see you too, Maggie," he said, hanging a halter on a crooked nail.

"If I may ask, where have you been all day?"

"You can ask if you like, but there isn't much I can say. Had to see a man about a myth."

"So General Sherman has you chasing hobgoblins again?"

Durken blinked. "Why would you say something like that?"

She gave him a humorless smile and tilted her head back. "You talk in your sleep, Durken. Who do you think sat by your bedside for two days after you were gored and while you lay in a delirium?" She pointed a finger at him. "You ought to leave it all alone and let the Devil handle what's his, or Sherman, although I can't say as I see much difference between them."

"I'd maybe agree with you, Maggie, except that there's a thing called duty."

"Duty to who? To some general who sees you like he sees a horse, or a cannon or a telegraph key? Somebody who uses you as a tool?"

"More duty to my friend. McAfee's out there right now, and I'm not going to let him twist in the wind wondering why I'm not helping him. As soon as I can ride, I'll join him."

Maggie went quiet, tears welling in her eyes.

Durken put his hands on her shoulders. "Maybe you'll understand what I'm gonna say, and maybe not. The things we fight are terrible, but if we don't fight them out there, we'll be fighting them here sooner or later, and they'll hurt a lot of people in between."

"But why you?"

"Because we get the job done."

XV

"**S**o, friend McAfee," said Willoughby, "Do you have a first name?"

"Not one I care to use."

"So, McAfee it is. My parents gave me a name that portended great things. I wonder sometimes whether they're looking down with disappointment from heaven or looking up with glee from hell."

The horses were keeping a leisurely pace as the shadows stretched from one horizon toward the other. The sky was a deep golden red as the sun dipped below the mountains ahead.

"Red sky at night, sailor's delight," said Willoughby.

"Yep," said McAfee. "Don't want a 'rosy-fingered dawn'."

"You've read Homer?"

McAfee nodded. "When I was a boy, I got a first rate Rhode Island grammar school education back in Providence. Old Mister Montrose was a terror to us all, but we learned what he taught us."

"Didn't spare the rod, eh?"

"I sure as hell wasn't spoiled. You said you were 'late of the Magnus Traveling Medicine Show.' Why aren't you with them now?"

"Quite a story." He took a moment to relight the cigar stub in his pipe. "For about three years, I traveled around with Doctor Magnus…that's what he called himself though he was no more a doctor than this horse. He sold Doctor Magnus' Miracle Elixir, guaranteed to cure warts, gout, palsy, rheumatism, neuralgia, chillblains, and a host of other maladies.

"I was part of the show. I'd stand in a pen and one of the doc's men would empty out a gunny sack full of rattlers into it, and I'd catch them with my bare hands, hold them up, play with them, walk around the pen and wave them at the rubes, and put them all back in the sack."

"Ever get bit?"

"More times than I could count." Willoughby pulled off his glove and showed McAfee the back of his hand, dotted with glossy patches of scar. "But of course, I milked them all dry of their venom before the show. That was my other job, collecting venom, which Magnus used as an ingredient in his elixir, never enough to do anybody any harm, but enough to make you feel the kick when you took a spoonful."

"And people took it, knowing that there was rattler venom in it?"

"Sure they did. There are lots of patent medicines that have venom in them, or say they do, like Metz and Knepp's Snake Venom Elixir. I suspect that most of them don't, but Magnus's Elixir was the real thing.

"We traveled all over for about three years, then one day, Magnus made a mistake mixing the elixir and put a little too much venom in it. Two people died in a small town in Texas, and their friends and relatives hunted us down a week later. If a sheriff hadn't shown up, they would have lynched us on the spot, but he took us to jail, and while we were waiting, Tate showed up."

"He gets around, doesn't he?"

Willoughby sucked on his pipe and let the smoke dribble from the corner of his mouth. "He talked to Magnus about the elixir, and he talked to me about the snakes and the venom. In the end, he found me more interesting and took me with him. He left Magnus in the Texas jail, and the next night, a lynch mob broke in and strung him up. I've been working for Tate ever since."

McAfee nodded. "Agent Tate seems unduly interested in things that kill people."

"That's so," said Willoughby. "How'd you run across him?"

"My partner and I were scouts for General Sherman in the war, and from time to time as situations develop with one tribe or another, he calls us in to handle things. About a year ago, the General brought us in to deal with an uprising. Tate stuck his snout in and damn near got it bitten off. I can't say I'm happy to see him again."

Willoughby chuckled. "I won't ask for details. I'm sure it's all 'classified.' That's Tate's favorite word; everything's a big secret. Yeah, Tate also has some favorite words for Sherman. You say you have a partner? Where is he, or is that classified too?"

"Durken's his name. He's recovering from an injury. I expect he'll be along, soon as he's able."

Willoughby turned to Cullison. "How much longer till we arrive, Sergeant?"

"Half an hour I'd say. You in a hurry, Willoughby?"

"No, just getting saddle sore. Seems nothing important ever happens in a town with a good hotel."

The party arrived at the camp as twilight set in. In a few moments, the quick darkness of flat land would swallow everything. Four tents were clustered around a cook fire. The horses were tethered close by, and McAfee could smell the pork and beans in the kettle.

"How far away is the wagon?" McAfee said.

"About a mile west," Cullison replied. "The Captain didn't think it was a good idea to camp too close in case there is a snake den nearby. We have a man on watch at the wagon, but the rest are here."

"If there's a den there, you could find another here, as easy," said Willoughby.

"Don't think for a minute we didn't walk every inch of this ground before we so much as put a stake in it."

They tied the horses and McAfee and Willoughby left their saddles and gear on Sweetheart for the moment. As they strolled into the circle of tents, the men, six soldiers, Tate, and Black, rose to their feet.

"What took you so long?" Tate said. "We've lost the light, and we'll have to wait 'til morning to go to the site."

Cullison gave Tate a stony look. "You don't run horses hard in this country unless you're chasing something, or it's chasing you. Your horse steps in a prairie dog hole and breaks a leg; it's a long walk home, Tate. Of course a city feller like you wouldn't know much about that, would you?"

No bond of friendship between those two, either, thought McAfee.

"Well, Tate," said Willoughby, "what matters is that we're here. Which accommodation is mine?"

Tate pointed to one of the canvas tents. "You and McAfee can share that one with Burns and McDunough. Sorry I can't give you a private room with bath."

"Quite all right, Tate. Working with you has made me used to privation."

Around the fire, the men shoveled supper into their mouths. One of the corporals, a rangy, hard-bitten veteran named Banks, said, around a mouthful of beans, "So you're the snake man, are you?"

"Yes, indeed. Titus Willoughby at your service, Corporal."

"You pick them up and handle them and all?"

"Just like house cats, my friend. It's all in knowing how."

"I had a boss once," said a private named Schmidt. "He owned a dairy farm in Pennsylvania. He gave us orders any time we found a rattler; we were to call him and keep an eye on it and not let it get away. We weren't allowed to kill them; he liked to do that himself. I guess it made me feel like a big man. He'd skin them and salt the hides; wore one as a hatband and had a bunch of them on the wall like paintings in frames.

"One afternoon, we were clearing some trees and we found a big old timber rattler stretched out on a flat rock the size of a mess table. He was at least six feet long, and almost as thick as my wrist. One of the men went for Sanger, the boss, and he came back with him carrying the garden hoe he kept sharpened like a hatchet.

"Sanger came close to the snake, and as soon as he got into range, it snapped back into a coil like somebody let go of a bedspring, and its rattles started chattering. Sanger took another step and jabbed at it with the end of the hoe, trying to get it to strike so he could chop off its head.

"That old snake was wily. It bobbed and weaved, but it didn't take the bait. Sanger misjudged its range. He got careless and stepped in too close, and that snake struck at him so fast, none of us could say when it moved. It grazed Sanger's pants leg but didn't break his skin. Sanger panicked and chopped at the rattler, and cut him in two about six inches below his head.

"The back end twisted and writhed for a minute, but the other part just lay still on its side and didn't move. Sanger was pretty shook up, but he tried to brave it out. He picked up the back end of the snake and pointed to the rattles. 'Look at those,' he said. 'This old boy's been around for a long time.'

"Then he crouched beside the head. He pointed at it. 'And look at those fangs. If you look close, you can see the poison sacs…'

"Just then, the rattler jerked around on that six inches of its spine and bit into Sanger's hand, right between his thumb and forefinger. The snake knew it was going to die, and it was playing possum, waiting for its chance for revenge."

"Oh, go on," said one of the other privates. "You expect us to believe that?"

"Hell, yeah," Schmidt protested. "I seen it myself,"

Banks turned to Willoughby. "What do you say, snake man?"

Willoughby smiled. "It could happen. Snakes are different from you and me. Cut one in two and the halves will live a while longer than we might." He turned to Schmidt. "Did Sanger die?"

"No, we sucked out the poison, but not 'til we had to cut the fangs out of his hand. They were locked in some kind of death grip. He had a V-shaped scar in his purlicue after that, as a reminder."

"Purlicue? What the hell's that?" said Cullison.

"The flesh between the thumb and forefinger," said Willoughby. "What in olden times people called the 'anatomical snuff box.'" He held his hand to his nose and sniffed in demonstration.

"How about you, Tate?" said Cullison. "Got any snake stories, or is that 'classified?'"

Tate glared at Cullison. "You can laugh if you want to, but I take my job seriously." He stood and went into his tent. Soon after, the rest of the men followed suit, except Schmidt, who pulled first watch, and the camp was quiet until dawn.

XVI

Durken lay in his bed and stared at the ceiling of the bunkhouse. Around him the other cowboys snored like hogs in rut. Lying around while McAfee was gone, maybe in danger, itched at him like his healing leg. "Aah, hell," he said, and threw off his blankets.

He dressed in the dark, pulled on his boots, and headed for the stable. Thunder stood in his stall and his ears perked up at the familiar low whistle. Durken backed Thunder out and slipped a bridle over his head. He threw a blanket over the bay's back and then his saddle.

"Well, boy, let's see if you can do it." Durken hesitated, wondering which might hurt worse or do more damage, putting his weight on his good leg and throwing the injured one over the saddle, or the reverse. After a minute's consideration and a slug of whiskey from his hip flask, he grabbed a handful of his trouser leg with one hand and the saddle horn with the other, put his foot in the stirrup and with a yank of his arm, threw his injured leg over Thunder's back.

Durken grunted in pain, and for a minute, he felt dizzy from it, then his head cleared, and he clucked his tongue. Thunder headed out of the stable at a slow gait into the moonlit yard and through the gateway. So far so good. Then he nudged the horse with his heels, and Thunder took off at a quick trot. Every bounce felt as if someone were poking his leg with an awl, but the longer he rode, the pain became an ache; then the ache became an itch, until he hardly felt it at all.

When he returned, Durken rode quietly into the yard and as he passed the Mansion, he saw a stout silhouette framed in the light from the open front door. There'd be no need for goodbyes in the morning.

It was still dark outside, and Durken was packing his saddlebags when Charlie came out of the kitchen. He had a small wrapped parcel in one hand and a larger one in the other. He raised the large one. "For your stomach." He raised the other. "For your leg."

"Much obliged, Charlie," he said, "I imagine both'll come in handy."

"You ride far?"

"Two days' worth give or take."

Charlie nodded to the smaller bundle. "Rub this ointment on the wound before you go to sleep, and when you get up in the morning. It will draw out the infection and make you heal faster." Charlie put a hand to Durken's forehead. "No fever now. That's good, but you take care of the leg, or it might come back."

Durken nodded. "I'll do that." He threw the saddlebags over his shoulder and headed for the stable. Under one arm he carried his Winchester, and under the other his .10 gauge, a reminder in case Tate forgot who was boss.

Durken lit a kerosene lamp that threw a dim yellow light across the stalls. In a few minutes, Thunder was saddled and Durken put his foot into the stirrup. He was about to throw his sore leg over the horse's back when a voice came from the shadows.

"So you were going to steal away like a thief in the night, Durken?" He peered into the semidarkness and saw Maggie's stout form sitting on a keg.

"Maggie, how long you been there?"

"All night. I saw you ride in and figured you'd be gone again by sunrise. Damn your eyes, Durken, you make me love you and hate you at the same time."

Durken didn't say anything for a moment, It was the first time that either of them had used the word "love" in their conversation, particularly about each other.

Maggie stood and crossed the floor. She put her hands on the cowboy's face and pulled it to her own and kissed him tenderly first, then hard and desperate. She pulled back, her face flushed in the lamplight. "You come back to me," she said, her voice breaking, and she turned and ran out the stable door into the night.

Durken stared after her for a while, then shook off his emotions and climbed onto Thunder. There was a job to be done. As he rode out of the yard, he looked back at the darkened mansion, and saw one flickering candle.

XVII

The ride to the attack site was a short haul, and no one said much in the chill of the morning. Tate and Black hung behind, holding a hushed conversation. The closer they came to the wagon, McAfee noticed that Sweetheart became a little skittish, planting each step with a degree of caution, as if one wrong move would bring them both down. The other horses looked to be picking their way as gingerly.

He rode up alongside Cullison. "Sergeant, have the horses behaved like this before, wary?"

"They don't like the place, if that's what you mean," Cullison said. "It's

…kissed him tenderly…then hard and desperate.

not exactly fear, but there's a sense of edginess about them."

"Maybe they know something we don't," Willoughby chimed in. "Animals have better sense than people about some things…the natural world, for instance. Or the unnatural."

"What do you mean?" McAfee said.

"Rattlers usually don't attack things they can't eat unless they're disturbed. You haven't seen Tate's pictures, have you?"

"He hasn't shown them to me, but there really hasn't been much time since we arrived. The General showed me one, though, those poor people, the Possets and their horses lying dead."

"Tate will show you the pictures taken of them the day after they were found. Both the man and the woman had over a hundred bites each, all over their bodies. Same for their horses. Rattlers usually don't strike something bigger than themselves over and over again. They pump in their venom and retreat. That being the case, there must have been a couple of hundred snakes in that nest, and I'm not so sure that running over their hole with a wagon wheel would provoke that many to action. It just doesn't seem right."

"Maybe they were having a camp meeting," said Cullison. "Wagon's right over that rise."

The Conestoga wagon, a long wooden trough topped with canvas stretched over half hoops, stood alone. The empty tongue protruded into the grass from the front, the reins and traces lying across it. A horse was tethered to the back of the wagon, but no one was in sight.

Cullison shouted, "Leary, where the hell are you?"

A corporal came around the wagon pulling up his trousers. He was a short man with stubby legs and arms, as if he were a plant that hadn't finished growing. "Heeding the call of Nature, Sarge." He tugged his suspenders over his shoulders.

"You're lucky one of those snakes didn't bite you in the ass. I know I wouldn't be sucking out the poison."

Leary grinned and McAfee saw that he was missing both upper front teeth. "No, but knowing you, you'd order somebody else to do it, just for sheer cussedness."

Tate rode up beside McAfee and Willoughby. "There's the wagon, men. See what you can find."

McAfee turned to Tate and eyed him for a few seconds before he spoke. "According to my orders from the General, I'm in charge 'in the field.' I don't know what that means to you, Tate, but to me it means I don't have to do a damned thing you say."

Tate flushed and his upper lip pulled back from his teeth, but he wasn't smiling. "You're out of your depth here, McAfee. You're not an investigator, you're a cowboy."

McAfee went on as if he hadn't spoken. "Now, I don't plan to abuse that authority, Tate, but if I were you, I wouldn't go throwing my weight around. You're lucky Durken's not here. I suspect he'd be a lot less diplomatic about it all."

Cullison eyed Tate then turned to McAfee. "Is that a fact? You're in charge of this show?"

McAfee patted his shirt pocket. "Got it in writing right here in the General's own hand." He pulled out Sherman's document and handed it to Cullison. Cullison's lips moved as he read each word. He handed back the paper to McAFee and said, "Yep, you're in charge all right...Lieutenant."

Tate's head jerked around as if he'd been slapped.

McAfee said, "Sergeant Cullison, if Agent Tate here gives you or any of your men an order to do something you think is out of line, check with me before you obey it."

Willoughby snickered, and Tate shot him a hard look.

"Come on, Willoughby. Let's see what we can see." McAfee nudged Sweetheart and rode toward the wagon.

The wagon looked the same as it had in the tintype Sherman had shown him, spoked wheels banded in iron held the driver's seat a good five feet off the ground. "Corporal, before I touch down, have you seen or heard any rattlers?"

Leary shook his head. "Nary a one. Of course, I've stayed on the wagon since I got here."

McAfee reached out and grabbed the wagon's brake lever. He stepped from the saddle directly onto one of the wheel spokes and climbed onto the hard wooden seat. He eyed a few dark spots that might have been blood, but none of them was bigger than a penny.

"If you're looking for blood, remember, people don't bleed from a snake bite like they do a bite from a bear." Willoughby had dropped to the ground. "The venom puckers the opening, and it helps keep the poison in the victim. That's why you have to cut them to get them to bleed. These poor souls never had that opportunity." Willoughby lit the stub in his pipe. "That and neither of them was wearing an emerald."

"An emerald? What for?"

Willoughby chuckled. "Just a superstition; if you wear an emerald, a snake won't bite you. Never been rich enough to test that theory."

McAfee nodded and stood on the seat to get a tall look at the ground around the wagon. "Sergeant, this isn't a road. I don't even see signs that other wagons have passed this way. How did these folks end up here?"

Cullison shrugged. "That I can't say. Maybe they thought going overland would give them a shortcut to Tolliver. It's about twelve miles northwest as the crow flies, but twenty miles or more the long way around on the road."

"Special Agent Tate." McAfee spoke without looking at him. "Would you please give me the pictures you haven't bothered to show me yet?"

"Black," Tate called, and the agent dismounted his horse. He pulled a package wrapped in paper from his saddlebag and brought it to the wagon. McAfee held out his hand, but Black waited for Tate to nod his head before he handed it over.

McAfee sat on the seat and unwrapped the package.

The first picture startled him. It showed Maria Posset laid out naked on a table, her darkened skin punctured by dozens of bites on every part of her body. Her eyes had been closed by some charitable soul, but attempts at pushing her tongue back into her gaping mouth were apparently futile. The most grotesque wound was a pair of fang marks through her right nipple, as if the rattler had been nursing at her breast.

"Not a pretty sight is it, McAfee?" said Tate, leaning casually against the wagon. "Now you see why the Service was called in."

McAfee eyed him coldly. "I don't know about the Secret Service, but I can guess why you are interested."

The second picture was of Reynald Posset, likewise displayed naked on the same table. He had more bites, if it were possible. No one had bothered to close his eyes.

"Ghastly," said Willoughby, craning his neck to see the stark image.

"You haven't seen these before?"

"No, all I got was a written description of the bodies. Doesn't do the horror justice."

The next picture was the one McAfee had seen in the General's car. He turned it in his hand, orienting it like a map to align the image to his perspective. "The feet of both bodies were turned north," he said. "Both are lying on their backs." He shuffled through the remaining pictures and didn't find what he wanted. "Tate, how many bites did the Possets have on their backs?"

"Not nearly so many. Most of them were on the front of the bodies."

"That makes it look as if they were facing the snakes and went over backwards when they were attacked." He shielded his eyes from the sun with his hand. "Sergeant, how far did your men look for the snake den?"

"A good three hundred yard radius from the wagon."

McAfee dropped to the ground and put his foot into Sweetheart's stirrup. "Let's try north. Willoughby, you and I will walk the horses through a quarter mile or so past that perimeter so we can get a good look at the ground. Sergeant, I'd say send two of your men along to ride about twenty yards from us on either side in case we run into any trouble."

"We're going along too," said Tate.

"No you're not. I don't want too many feet damaging whatever sign may still exist. You and Black stay here."

"I'm not going to…"

"Sergeant Cullison, if these men attempt to do anything contrary to my orders, please restrain them."

Cullison grinned. "Yes, sir."

"Come on, Willoughby. Let's go find some snakes."

XVIII

Durken reined Thunder to a stop as he arrived at the crossroads with a sign pointing east toward Portman and the number eighteen. He had ridden more slowly than usual, favoring his leg, but he realized that he'd have to pick up his pace if he was going to make it to the town before dark. He wasn't afraid of being out alone, but the thought of sleeping with that sore leg on the cold ground because Portman was closed for the night had no appeal at all.

He'd seen few travelers on the road, a pair of cowboys on horseback and three supply wagons with tired-looking teamsters headed west. No one going his direction, although someone riding at a normal pace would overtake him sooner or later. It was as if people knew better than to ride east, where the sun goes down sooner.

Durken clucked his tongue. "Ho." Thunder set off at a trot. He flicked the reins, and the horse sped its pace. The bouncing brought back the ache which had almost subsided in Durken's leg, and he gritted his teeth. He reached into his duster for his flask and poured a slug of whiskey down his throat. It burned the whole way down, but by the time it landed in his stomach, it seemed to ease the pain a little.

What Seven Stars had told him about the Ki-no Na-te seemed farfetched, but the details of the myth seemed to fit what he'd seen in the tintype. A mass of snakes big enough to swarm over two adults and two horses and bite them to death acting with one purpose stood against everything he knew on the subject. Another consideration was the missing girl and the story's detail about sacrifices.

He and McAfee had known Seven Stars for a long time, and they had stood shoulder to shoulder with him against some eerie forces. The blind chief knew as much about gods and demons and such maybe as anyone alive, and he'd never steered the cowboys wrong. If Durken were a church-going man, he might have prayed, like a knight going on a holy crusade, but he was a man who relied on his wits, his strength, and his guns, all of which had kept him alive so far, and he saw no sense in changing his ways now. Whatever was out there, he and McAfee would take it on face-to-face.

XIX

McAfee and Willoughby dismounted at a distance from the wagon. Banks and Schmidt sat astride their mounts to either side. Willoughby took a small leather pouch from his coat and opened the drawstring. He poured a yellow powder from it into his hand and rubbed it on his boots. He offered the pouch to McAfee. "Sulfur. For some reason the snakes don't like it."

McAfee rubbed the powder on his boots. "Why's that, I wonder?"

"Maybe it reminds them of their Satanic origin."

"You believe that?"

"Hell, no," Willoughby said with a laugh, "because they don't like cinnamon oil, clove oil, or cedar oil, either, but out here I use sulfur because those other things are in such short supply."

"I read in some book once they don't much care for garlic, either."

"I've heard that too, but I never tested that theory."

McAfee looked across the expanse of wiry grass. "In the pictures, none of this was flattened down, but we don't know exactly how long these people were dead before they were found. Grass could've sprung back up by then."

"You're thinking something else was involved in this besides the rattlers?"

"Maybe. I don't know for sure."

"More things in heaven and earth, eh?"

"Yep. Besides, as many snakes as bit up the Possets, you'd think they'd've pushed the grass down a little, attacking in a mass like that."

"I doubt that. You've heard people talk about a 'snake in the grass?' I'd say they'd just push this buffalo grass aside slithering through it."

McAfee nodded. "You'd know better than I do. I suppose our best move is to criss-cross this area in ten-foot sweeps and see what we find. We'll walk the horses with us. Like you said, they seem to have a sense of things that ain't right."

"As you say." Willoughby took a thin pole as long as his leg from a scabbard on his saddle. At its end was a two-pronged fork.

"You gig them with that stick?"

Willoughby shook his head. "No, you pin the snake to the ground with it, and then you can decide what to do with it next."

"I guess that's all right if they come at you one at a time."

To that, Willoughby had no answer.

The search was tedious but necessary, pacing back and forth across a hundred feet, looking closely through the grass for any opening or sign, then advancing twenty feet. The sun grew higher and hotter, then started working its way toward the horizon. They stopped for a moment. McAfee rolled a cigarette and Willoughby wiped his face with a kerchief. "How much longer are we going to do this?"

"As long as it takes. Those snakes came from someplace, and I expect if we keep looking, we're gonna find it."

XX

Durken made better time than he thought, and he arrived in Portman way before sundown. He quartered Thunder at the ramshackle barn that passed for a livery stable and started up the boardwalk toward the Portman Hotel. Two cowboys were walking in the opposite direction, one a tall, broad shouldered man with a thick four-and-eight moustache. The other was a stout fellow with eyes as wide apart as a trout on either side of his big, sunburned nose.

They passed Durken, staring straight ahead as if they were looking at something in the distance. He turned as they did, trying to remember. The name...Martin. Hank Martin.

"Hey, fellows." Durken called to them, and they walked on as if he hadn't spoken. "Hey, Hank." The men hesitated for a second, as if they might turn around, then kept walking. "Hey, Hank Martin."

The cowboys stopped and turned slowly. Durken caught up to them. "You Hank Martin?" The question seemed to take the man with the moustache by surprise. The other fellow's eyes wandered a little then seemed to focus, which was a chore since he was so wall-eyed. The tall man closed his eyes and opened them, and then he said, "Uh, yeah, I'm Hank Martin."

"Then you must be Ed Durst."

They looked at each other then back to Durken, but slow, as if they were waking from slumber. "Do we know you?" said Durst.

"No, but I met your buddy Jake Ketchum a few days ago. He's been looking for you two." He turned to Martin. "Your sister is worried sick, afraid you're dead. You might send them a telegram and let them know you're all right."

"Yes. A telegram." They turned away from Durken and went on their way like men wading in chest-deep water. Durken hoped the telegraph office hadn't closed for the day. He wasn't sure what was up with Martin and Durst, but it didn't look as if Martin would be sending a telegram any time soon.

The telegraph operator was a thin, balding man named Briggs. The first thing Durken noticed when he walked into the telegraph office was a Union officer's cap and a saber decorating the wall behind the counter. The second thing he noticed was Briggs's empty shirt sleeve pinned up to his right shoulder.

"What can I do for you, cowboy?" Briggs said with an affable grin.

"What you do for most people, I suppose."

Briggs set a sheet of paper on the counter and took the stub of a pencil from behind his ear. "Recipient?"

"You mean who's it going to?" Durken said. Briggs nodded. "Sheriff Harvey Bennet, Bacon Rock, Nevada."

Briggs jotted down the information. "Message?

"Ketchum's friends..."

"That's K-E-T-C-H-U-M?"

"I guess so. Ketchum's friends alive well Portman."

Briggs raised an eyebrow. "These men wanted for anything?"

"Nope. Relative's looking for one of them is all.

Briggs nodded. "Signature?"

"D-U-R-K-E-N."

"I'll send it right away. At fifty cents a word, that'll be three dollars."

As Durken counted out the coins, he said, "What unit were you in?"

"Third Massachusetts. You?"

"I rode with Sherman through Georgia."

"Looks like you came out of it better than I, friend."

"Sometimes war gives you hurt that doesn't show on the outside."

Briggs pondered that thought and said, "I see your point. Well, Mister Durken, if you want to wait for an answer, I can keep the office open a while. It's the least I can do for a fellow veteran"

"No need. It's just information. I don't expect a conversation."

As Durken turned to go, Briggs said, "You know, sometimes I'll feel an itch in that missing arm, and there's nothing to scratch. I expect it's just as bad or worse when you're missing a piece of your soul."

"You got that right."

XXI

The sun had nearly set when Willoughby spotted the rock and the dark opening underneath. "McAfee, here." He waved a beckoning hand and pointed to the ground in front of him. Banks and Schmidt became suddenly attentive, but Willoughby told them, "Hold where you are."

A flat slab of limestone broke the surface of the ground like the edge of a coin, as if it had been pushed upward from beneath. Below the lip of the stone, an opening showed, barely wide enough for a man to slip through, but accommodating enough for a snake.

McAfee walked all around the crescent of stone. "What do you think, Willoughby? Is this the den?"

"Could be." He walked around for a moment looking at the ground until he found a rock the size of his fist. He threw it into the opening, and they heard it thump and clatter for a second or two, then silence. "Sounds like a cave. That's stone on the floor, not soil. No rattles, so I guess this isn't it."

"Hold up a minute," McAfee said. "All around this rock there's grass growing right up to the edge. There's bare earth around the opening. Something's been coming and going enough to wear away the grass."

"But it's not there now. That makes no sense. Rattlesnakes don't migrate. Where'd they go?"

"I don't know, but it would be interesting to find out." He crouched to get a better look into the hole. He reached under the lip and his fingers found deep angular grooves cut into the stone. "There's something carved under here." He lay down and rolled onto his back. The stone was cut with the symbol of an arrow aimed outward, but instead of a straight line, the six-inch shaft was curved in an S, and instead of the angular fletching projecting from the shaft, short, straight lines crossed it.

"Willoughby, you got a piece of paper and a pencil?"

Willoughby tore a leaf from his notebook and handed it and a pencil to McAfee. "I'm going to take a rubbing of this, and then…" Thunder whinnied. From the corner of his eye, McAfee saw a glimpse of movement and instinctively twisted aside as a rattlesnake struck at him. Willoughby thrust his snake stick at it and pinned the thrashing serpent to the ground, its rattles whirring.

"Sweet Jesus," said McAfee, jackknifing himself into a sitting position and staring at the snake. "That was close. Where the hell did he come from?"

"The question is, why didn't he rattle before he struck?"

McAfee stood up and backed away from the opening. Willoughby dropped to his haunches and peered at the snake through the bottom of his spectacles. "He's six feet if he's an inch."

"Can you tell how old he is by counting the rattles, maybe tell me how long he's been down there?"

"I'm afraid it doesn't quite work that way," Willoughby said, "All the number of rattles can tell us is how many times the snake has shed his skin. That happens when they outgrow the old one, and the process slows down as they get older. But our friend here has been around a good while, I'd say."

Willoughby pulled a long, thin knife from a sheath on his belt and with one quick slash, severed the rattler's head from its body. The hind part of the snake, still pinned by the fork, twisted and thrashed, nearly tying itself into a knot. He waited until the body stopped writhing and scooped it and the head into a stiff leather pouch. "We'd better get back to camp. I'm not sure I want to be around here after dark."

XXII

"Any of you ever see a symbol like this?" Tate passed McAfee's drawing to the corporal on his left, and the paper went from hand to hand around the fire circle. One by one the soldiers looked at the picture and shook their heads.

"It must be of some importance, for someone to carve it into the rock. Maybe it's a tribal symbol of some kind," Black said.

"Well, McAfee," said Tate, "you're the Indian expert here. What do you make of it?"

"Since we're looking for snakes, it makes sense that the arrow is curvy. And since we're looking for rattlers, it makes sense that instead of the back angled fletching; the arrow has straight lines across the end, like the rattles on a snake's tail."

"The arrow head suggests that the snake is a weapon to be aimed at a target," said Willoughby. "That's a sobering thought."

"Maybe someone found a way to control the snakes," Tate said, "make them attack on command."

"And maybe that's why you're here," McAfee said. "You want that know-how for yourself."

Tate bristled. "I'm following the orders of the President."

"Then why does my authority trump yours? Does Ulysses S. Grant even know you're out here or what you're doing? Does he want to sic a mess of snakes on some enemy? Or maybe does the Secret Service want it for themselves in case it might come in handy?"

"You're out of line. I don't have to debate this with you, McAfee."

"No you don't, but you would if you thought you could win."

"Gentlemen," Willoughby interrupted, "there's one other aspect of that symbol we haven't discussed yet, the way the arrow points. It doesn't direct snakes into the cave, it directs them out."

"I guess there's only one thing for us to do," McAfee said. "Go in that hole in the ground tomorrow and see what's under that rock."

XXIII

Durken found the Portman Hotel's accommodations every bit as comfortable as McAfee had. The mattress felt as if it were filled with river stones, and the pillow with sand. He lay on the bed in the candlelight and rubbed Charlie's ointment into the healing gash in his leg. It didn't hurt nearly as much as Durken thought it might, but he figured he'd pay for the day's ride in the morning.

He blew out the candle and was asleep before the cockroaches had the nerve to creep out of the woodwork.

The morning proved Durken right. Every time he bent his leg at the knee, a burning pain shot through it. Charlie's ointment helped a little, but descending the stairs to the hotel's main floor stabbed him with every step.

Breakfast, ham and eggs and coffee, was better than he expected, but he supposed that the Portman Hotel had to offer something better than its beds to stay in business. Durken limped to the livery to fetch Thunder, paid the grizzled three-toothed codger who ran the place, and took a minute to decide how to get into the saddle.

A box stood in a corner near the doors, and Durken considered using it to ease his mount, but he saw the old coot watching him with a slack-jawed grin. He gritted his teeth, put his foot in the stirrup and saddled up. It hurt like hell, and Durken drew in a sharp breath, but he didn't show weakness.

As he rode out of Portman, he passed the town pump. Martin and Durst stood beside it, and as he rode by, they followed him with their eyes, and then with a turn of their heads, and then with a turn of their feet. Durken didn't look back, but he could feel their gaze on him like something cold and slippery up and down his spine until he was past the edge of town.

XXIV

"Do you have any experience with caves?" Willoughby said, as they rode across the grassland to the opening they'd found the day before. McAfee, Tate, Willoughby, and Schmidt and Banks, the two soldiers who had ridden out with them yesterday, rode six abreast, including the pack mule with equipment.

"I had some; one summer when I was a boy in Rhode Island, my family went to the seashore at Newport, and my father took my brother Russell and me to see what they called the Pirates' Caves. He was a Providence policeman, and he was interested in them because stories had it that pirates, especially Captain Kidd used some of the caves to hide himself and his loot. Some of them were just holes in the ground. One, you could row a boat into at high tide."

"So, it didn't bother you going underground?"

"No, we had candles and a lantern, Russell and I had a fine time."

"That's good to know. Fifty feet underground's no place to find out you're claustrophobic."

"That's a new word for me. What's it mean?"

"Afraid of being closed in. How about you Tate?"

"I've never been in a cave, but I've been in plenty of closed up places, vaults and such. I won't have a problem."

McAfee had grudgingly agreed, at Willoughby's request, to include Tate in the expedition, although he still had reservations about the man's trustworthiness. He would have preferred to have Durken watching his back, but some days, what you want and what you get don't match up.

Willoughby had carefully examined the snake he had killed the day before and found nothing unusual. He pronounced it a common rattlesnake native to the region, and said it had no physical abnormalities. The snake's odd behavior, striking without sounding a warning first, was a puzzle, though, and something McAfee hoped wasn't a trend.

The opening looked the same as it had yesterday, the dark showing under a crescent of sun-baked stone. Willoughby took three small kerosene lanterns from a bulky bag on the pack mule.

"Wouldn't open flame be better? Snakes are afraid of fire aren't they?" Tate said.

"Snakes don't see well," Willoughby answered. Their vision works more on movement. Light is light to them, sun, fire, or candle. They might pull back from the heat of a fire, but a torch small enough to take through that opening crevice wouldn't make much difference." He pulled on thick leather gauntlets yellowed with sulfur. "I'll go in first and see where that opening leads and whether there's room for more than one of us at a time."

Willoughby lit the lantern and held it into the opening. He closed one eye and peered into the darkness with the other. "When you two go in, close one eye for a minute so it'll adjust to the darkness more quickly." Willoughby tied a rope to his ankle and handed the other end to Tate.

"Pull me out if I holler for help." He set the lantern down and dropped to his stomach.

"You're not going to crawl into that hole head first are you?" Tate said.

"My eyes aren't in my knees, Tate. I don't want to poke my legs blind into a snake burrow. I need to see what's in front of me." As he pushed the lantern ahead of him, Willoughby's head and shoulders disappeared under the rock, then his hips, then his feet.

In a minute they heard him say, "It widens out a few feet in, and it's a gentle slope, but it's still a low ceiling." Willoughby's voice sounded as if his head were in a rain barrel. "I'm going a little further to see whether this opens up into a chamber."

Willoughby didn't say a word for a while, but the rope kept disappearing under the rock. Finally, it stopped. "There's a room down here and a couple of tunnels branching off." His voice sounded very far away, although he hadn't pulled the whole fifty feet of the rope. "Come on down."

"After you," McAfee said to Tate, gesturing to the dark hole.

Tate looked around him, as if he were taking a last look at life before jumping off a cliff, lit his lantern, and crawled into the crevice.

"Should we tether the horses?" Banks said. "You might be a while."

"Maybe you could stay in the saddle and hold their reins. You know what we're looking for. If a mess of snakes came boiling out of the ground, I'd hate to be tied to a stake."

Banks nodded. "Whatever you say."

From below, Tate called out. "I'm here. Come on, McAfee."

McAfee closed one eye and set his lantern down. He drove a peg attached to a spool of cord into the ground just outside the hole."Ariadne's clew," he said, and threw the spool into the opening.

McAfee took a deep breath and crawled into the darkness.

He found himself inching downward between two vast slabs of tawny limestone. Caves he'd been in before had sandy floors, not stone. He turned the lantern to one side and the other and saw the gap diminish in the distance at either hand. The crevice seemed to extend forever. He took in a breath and smelled a dry earthy scent suffused with a bitter tang.

It was slow going, pushing with his knees and pulling with his elbows on the rough, hard stone. Ahead, he saw a faint glow of light. "Turn yourself around and come in feet first," said Willoughby, his voice seeming to come from everywhere. "There's a drop of about four feet when you get to the chamber. You won't want to land on your face."

McAfee twisted to his right and gradually reversed his position. He now had to push with his forearms and inch down, dragging the lantern behind him, until he felt his feet go over a lip in the rock.

"Go ahead and give yourself a shove. You'll drop right to the floor."

McAfee did, and instead of landing on a hard rock surface, he found what felt like damp leaves under his boots. He looked down and what he saw on the floor of the chamber was a cushion of translucent white snake skins, hundreds of them. McAfee shuddered in spite of himself.

Willoughby said, "I think we found the den."

XXV

Durken rode into Casselman just after noon. He figured he'd find McAfee and the others if he asked at the telegraph office where there were soldiers camped nearby. If that failed, he'd try the local storekeeper and the bartenders. Someone in that range would surely know.

The saloon looked to be the best bet to start. Durken was hungry and thirsty from the ride, and a little whiskey would dull the ache in his leg. The building called Saloon looked to be a few notches lower than the Silver Dollar back home, but whiskey was whiskey wherever you went.

The bartender had little to distinguish him from the patrons. Where Liam wore a shiny vest over shirtsleeves and a silk necktie like a chrysanthemum, the saloon's bartender wore the same nondescript flannel shirt and canvas trousers as most of the cowboys standing at the bar or sitting at one of the round tables.

"What'll you have?" Also, unlike Liam, his teeth were yellow, turning to brown.

"Whiskey. Bring me the bottle."

He nodded and came back with a green bottle and a glass. Durken put a five dollar gold piece on the bar and uncorked the bottle. The tumbler looked as if it might have been washed once, but maybe not. He poured three fingers of whiskey into it and swirled it around, figuring the alcohol would kill anything that might hurt him, if it didn't kill him in the bargain.

Durken was filling his flask from the bottle when the bartender came back. "You want anything else? Food maybe?"

Durken eyed a cockroach strolling casually up the bar as if it owned the place. He shook his head. "No food, but maybe you can tell me if there are soldiers camped nearby. I need to meet up with them."

"I think we found the den."

The barkeep shook his head. "There've been some soldiers in here the last few days, but I can't say where to find them."

A tall cowboy with hair falling over a droopy eyelid spoke up. "I seen a camp about four miles east of town, a little ways off the road."

"That might be it. Much obliged." Durken pushed the bottle in his direction. "Pour yourself one." He did, and Durken corked the bottle, tucked it under his arm, and walked out of the dingy saloon.

Climbing back onto Thunder hurt, but a little less. Maybe it was the rotgut brew from the bottle. Durken clucked his tongue and soon, Casselman faded behind him.

Tate dug the toe of his boot into the mass of snake skins and kicked some away. There were more underneath, but old and desiccated. "Looks as if this den's been in business quite a while."

"I wouldn't go kicking around things, even dead ones, if I were you, Tate," Willoughby said. "There's too much about this business that isn't ordinary, and I'd rather know what we're dealing with before we act." He turned to McAfee. "Three tunnels. You're in charge. Which one first?"

All three tunnels were tall enough and wide enough for a man to walk through them at a crouch. McAfee wet his thumb and stepped to each of the openings in turn. He pointed to the middle one. "Air's moving through this one. It may be another way out. We might be safer in this one first, see what's down here instead of starting with one of the dead end tunnels where we might be cornered."

"Middle it is," said Willoughby. He turned up the flame of his lantern and stepped into the passage. Like the chamber, the floor was carpeted with rattlesnake skins, and Willoughby was careful to walk flat-footed to avoid disturbing them. The walls were smoother than McAfee expected, and he said so.

"This cave was likely formed by water flowing through faults in the stone back when this whole part of the country was under an inland sea," said Willoughby. "The water eroded the softer layer of stone below the hard one. The sea dried up, and left what you see here. It's a dry cave now, no dripping water, and that's why we don't see any stalactites, icicle-shaped formations hanging overhead. It's cool and dry, comfortable for snakes."

"You say this was all under water once?" Tate asked.

"You can believe science, or if you prefer, believe the story of Noah. Either way, yes it was." The further they went into the passage, the less Willoughby's voice boomed and echoed.

McAfee carried his lantern at his side rather than in front of him, and looked back every few steps to make sure nothing was coming up behind them. He was still holding the spool loosely in his hand and paying out the white cord as he went. leaving a trail back out of the accursed place.

Ahead, a grey light shone into the passage. "Gentlemen, we've reached the end of the road." Willoughby turned to the side, so that Tate and McAfee could see past him. The passage dead-ended and joined a narrow chimney that showed daylight about thirty feet overhead. McAfee tilted his head back and studied the chimney. "I don't think we'll climb out of here that way."

"No," said Willoughby. "It's too narrow, but I imagine snakes would find it convenient."

"That's where they went?" said Tate.

"One possibility," Willoughby answered. "Let's turn around and take a look at the other two tunnels."

The left-hand tunnel sloped downward and became progressively lower until the men couldn't even crawl through it. "Hush," said Willoughby, "and don't move. Listen."

From a distance, McAfee heard the echoing drip of water. "Must be a spring empties down there."

"That explains in part, at least, how the snakes could survive here. Let's back out of here and try the last tunnel."

The right-hand tunnel was level, much like the center one, but instead of running forward in a straight line, it twisted and wound like the serpents that had lived in it. Willoughby turned a corner in the passage and stopped suddenly. "My Lord."

He stepped from the passage into a domed room at least twenty feet in diameter, the floor hollowed out into a crater overflowing with bones. The charnel pit held all sizes and shapes, from the delicate bones of mice and rats to the thick, heavy bones of cattle and horses, and among them human skulls.

"That one's a child," said Tate, leaning over the edge of the pit to retrieve it. He held it in his hand, studying it in the light of his lamp.

"Sophia Posset?" said McAfee?

Tate shook his head, "No, her skull would be fresh. This one's been down here for a long time."

"Look up there," said Willoughby, pointing across the room. Carved into the wall and pointing upward was the symbol, the serpentine arrow, as big as a man. No one spoke for a time, then Willoughby broke the silence. "My advice is we go back to the surface. Our lamps will run low soon. I don't want to be fumbling around down here in the dark."

"No argument here," McAfee said. "Tate?"

Tate threw the skull back into the pit. "I've seen enough. Let's go."

The climb out of the cave was easier and faster than the descent into it. Banks and Schmidt had secured Willoughby's rope, and all three used it to pull themselves out of the crevice. As they shook the dust from their clothes, Willoughby said, "More things, Horatio."

McAfee nodded. "To tell the truth, I'm happy to see the sun again."

"You can say that for me, too," Tate threw in.

"I'm surprised you agree with him."

All three turned and saw Durken sitting astride Thunder. He grinned and said, "What'd I miss?"

Within a half hour, the party found the hole where the chimney opened to the surface.

"Like most animals, it looks as if they instinctively left a getaway for themselves." Willoughby crouched and peered into the hole. McAfee hunkered down beside him and felt the draught of cool air breeze past his face.

"Seems as if it might take a while for a couple hundred snakes to climb out of there."

"Not if they're moving *en masse*. The ones below would push the others up and out of the hole like water from a fountain."

"There's something to have a nightmare over," Tate said. "So what do we do?"

"One thing we could do is plug the holes," Willoughby said. "Keep them from getting back into the den, since we know they're gone now."

"And if they come back?"

Willoughby shrugged. "Hard to tell. If they come back, they'll be in the open and maybe we can use a grass fire to burn the lot."

"Sounds as if it might work," said McAfee. "How do we close the openings?"

Willoughby turned to Cullison. "Sergeant, do you have any explosives at your post?"

Cullison nodded. "We got some dynamite. I can send a man to get it and bring it back quick enough." He turned to McAfee, who nodded. Tate frowned but didn't argue.

"Well, that's it then," Willoughby said. "We'll post a guard for the night, and in the morning, we'll close up their hidey-hole."

"And what if they come back overnight?" Durken said.

Willoughby smiled around the stem of his pipe. "So much the better. We'll cave it in on them, and that should be the end of it."

McAfee left Banks and Schmidt to watch the opening with the promise of relief before nightfall and orders to mount and run at the first sign of trouble. McAfee's words were, "At the first sign of a snake, tear the hell out of here." They built a fire at the mouth of the cave and one at the chimney and watched both entrances from fifty feet away.

Back at camp, McAfee and Durken sat out of earshot to discuss everything that had happened. Durken told McAfee the legend Seven Stars had shared with him. "That part about the snakes attacking in an army sounds like what happened to the Possets."

"Sacrificing a child every new moon is what worries me. If the Patapa cult is back in business, they are a real threat."

"You believe in that Snake Mother stuff, the Ki-no Na-te? You think she's real?"

"Doesn't matter what I believe. What matters is what the Patapa believe. If they think she's real, they'll do whatever the legend says."

"But how do you figure the snakes attacking all at once?"

"I don't know how it happened, but I know for sure that it did. What I saw in that cave convinced me."

"There's another thing; remember that fellow was looking for his friends?"

"You mean Ketchum?"

"Yep. I ran into the pair of them in Portman. But there was something wrong. You remember those men in the unit the doctors gave laudanum when they were shot or lost a limb?"

McAfee nodded.

"Martin and Durst both had those same empty eyes, as if they'd just taken a hefty dose."

"Maybe that's why they didn't meet up with Ketchum. Maybe they developed the habit."

"That's possible, but they might have a time finding it out on the trail."

McAfee nodded. "Another mystery, as if we didn't have enough already."

"Damn."

"Yep."

Durken uncapped his flask and offered it to McAfee, who took a long pull. "Here comes Cullison."

The sergeant was walking toward them at a pretty good clip with a paper in his hand and a worried look on his face. "What do you make of him?" said Durken.

McAfee shrugged. "You and I have known and lot of sergeants in our time."

Durken nodded. "Yeah, and?"

"And he's one of them."

Cullison waited until he stood right in front of the cowboys before he spoke. "My men came back with the dynamite." McAfee had told him from the beginning to forego the usual protocols concerning rank, saluting, sirring and such, and just call them by their last names, same as the ranch hands, and do what he and Durken told him. "There was a telegram at the outpost for you, McAfee." He held out the paper.

"Did you read it?"

He flushed. "Couldn't help but read it. Same for the men who went for the dynamite. It's from the General."

McAfee unfolded it and held it so Durken could read it as well. The message was terse: Another incident. Collinsville. Investigate. Sherman.

"How far is Collinsville from here?" Durken said.

"About forty miles north. Not much to it, really. There was a copper mine for a while, but it played out and the town pretty much folded."

"That's a surprise," said McAfee. I recall reading in some book that there are big deposits of copper all around this territory."

"Pit mine or tunnels?" said Durken.

"It's an underground mine," said Cullison, "but I can see what you're headed for."

"Not a cave," said McAfee, rolling a cigarette, "but a hole in the ground just the same."

Durken offered the flask to Cullison who looked grateful for a drink. "I'd say we oughta start for there at first light. We'll take Willoughby, Tate and Black, and two of your riders. The rest of you can take care of that den."

Cullison nodded. "We'll close it up good."

No one spoke for a minute. "You know, this territory used to be a pretty good assignment. Just a few redskins and coyotes to deal with. Now it's all gone to hell."

McAfee lit his cigarette. He took a deep drag and let out a cloud of smoke. "You know what, Cullison? That might be closer to the truth than you think."

XXVI

"**Y**ou know, McAfee, Willoughby may have spoken too soon about dynamiting the cave." Tate and Black sat beside them by the campfire. "As I recall, when you were fresh out of the ground, you didn't seem to think it was such a bad idea."

"We may be destroying evidence. Those bones, for example."

McAfee eyed him coldly. "What you mean to say is we may be destroying some clue as to how somebody might be controlling the snakes and using them as a weapon."

"Of course. How can we fight against something like that if we don't know how it's done?"

Durken pointed an accusing finger at Tate. "And how could the Secret Service use it against some enemy if you don't find out how to do it yourselves?"

"That symbol for another thing," Tate said, ignoring Durken's accusation. "What does it mean? Is it a command, a protection, what? We may never know if you blow the place up."

Durken turned to Black. "Agent Black, are you in agreement with Tate?"

Black said, "Washington gives him orders, he follows them. He gives me orders, I follow them. It's not up to me to question."

"'Theirs not to reason why, theirs but to do and die,'" McAfee said. "You left out one link in the chain, Black."

"What's that?"

McAfee patted Sherman's letter in his shirt pocket. "Out here, 'in the field,' Durken and I give orders, and you two follow them. And the order stands. Tomorrow the cave is sealed."

Tate sprang to his feet. "Fine. Do that. Dynamite the snake den, you stubborn son of a bitch. And you can have all the grief that's going to rain down because of it."

McAfee grinned. "It goes with the territory, Tate. No, actually, it is the territory."

Tate turned on his heel and stormed off to the tent with Black close behind him.

"You're enjoying this, aren't you?" Durken said stretching his aching leg toward the warmth of the fire.

"Not as much as you might think. Things'd go a lot smoother if we were all on the same side of this argument."

"But at least we know Cullison and his men will do what we say instead of what Tate says."

"That's true, and it's a comfort." McAfee looked toward the tent. "But I'm still not leaving those two behind to interfere. I want Tate and Black where I can see them."

What Durken and McAfee didn't see were the dark forms of Durst and Martin crouching in the tall grass beyond the circle of firelight. They weren't close enough to hear all that was said, but they heard enough. As if on a signal, the pair turned away and stole into the night.

XXVII

In the morning, the party saddled their horses. Tate watched as Durken limped to Thunder and stiffly threw himself into the saddle. "You sure you're up to this, Durken? You look like you couldn't fight three whores and win."

"Seeing just you and Black there, that makes only two, but I'm still willing if you want to test that theory." Durken laughed. Tate didn't. "Cullison!"

"Yeah, Durken?" the sergeant called from the other side of the camp.

"We'll see you in Collinsville tomorrow or the next day."

"Yep."

"Let's ride." Durken clucked his tongue, and Thunder led the group across the dew-wet grass to the road, including the two privates Cullison sent along, Biggs and Evans.

Cullison found Schmidt lashing the case of dynamite to the pack mule. "You ready to move out?"

"Sure thing, Sergeant."

Cullison raised his voice. "Let's go, boys. The sooner we close up that snake hole, the better."

The soldiers mounted their horses and headed for the mouth of the cave. The guards were still on duty, and the fires were still burning at the entrance and the chimney. A corporal named Barnes sat astride his horse at the entrance.

"You in a hurry to go somewhere, Barnes?" Cullison said.

"No, Sergeant, but I heard what those men found down below, and I figured I was better off ready to ride if any snakes showed up. I've been in the saddle all night."

"Well, you can climb down now. We have work to do."

None of the men was eager to volunteer to go below and set the charges, so Cullison let them draw straws for the honor. Banks won, if you call it winning. The plan was to set dynamite at the mouths of the three passages that branched off below, and after they were caved in, collapse the crevice and the chimney.

Banks crawled between the layers of limestone, pushing his lantern ahead of him and dragging a canvas rucksack filled with dynamite behind. As he edged downward, he paid out fuse from a spool. More than once, he stopped to listen for any tell-tale sound, ready to yell to the surface for the men to haul him up by the rope tied to his ankle. Nothing. The cave below was perfectly silent. He looked to one side then the other, shining his lantern, and saw nothing but the layers of tawny limestone retreating into black infinity.

He reached the bottom of the crevice and turned himself around as Willoughby had instructed so that he landed feet first. The spongy feel of the snake skins under his boots made him shudder, and he hesitated a long moment to bend over to untie the rope from his ankle.

The rucksack held twelve sticks of dynamite and blasting caps to do the tunnels. Four for each. Banks worked quickly, afraid that at any second, a fanged head would strike from the darkness of some corner, or spring up from the mass of skins that littered the cave floor, but none did. He wedged the dynamite sticks into crevices in the rock and set the caps and fuses. These he tied into the main fuse leading from above.

"Okay, I'm coming up." Banks clambered out of the chamber and lay face down on the flat limestone of the crevice.

"Come on," shouted Cullison, whose voice seemed a world away. "Grab the rope. We'll haul you out."

Banks wrapped the rope a couple of turns around his wrist and gripped it with both hands. "All right. I'm ready. Get me the hell out of here." He felt a sharp tug at his wrist, and he began to slowly slide upward toward the surface.

Then he heard it, a whisper at first, but louder by the second; a mix of rustling, hissing, and the whirring of rattles. Banks turned his head and shined the lantern between the limestone layers to his right and saw in the distance, the glittering gems of hundreds of eyes reflecting the lantern's glow.

"They're coming! Mother of God, get me out of here!" Banks screamed.

On the surface, Cullison thought fast and whipped a loop of the rope around the horn of one of the horses' saddles. He slapped the animal on the rump and it took off running, dragging Banks to the surface, and with him, a writhing mass of rattlesnakes, fangs in his flesh.

The men rushed forward to try to help Banks, but before they could, a slithering sea of fanged horrors surged from the opening. The snakes struck at the men and horses, twined themselves around blue-clad legs and climbed the bodies that swung frantic arms to knock them away.

Cullison winced as a rattler sank its fangs into his thigh and another into his arm. He pulled his Colt revolver and blew the head from the one at his wrist and aimed for the one on his leg, but another struck his gun hand and he dropped the pistol. Here's where I die, he thought, but before he lost consciousness, he staggered to the embers of the nearby fire, snakes swinging from him like vines in the wind.

The sergeant thrust his hand into the dying fire and grabbed a stick of charred, smoking wood. The pain of his burning flesh would have made him drop it, but his hand was already numb from the venom the snakes were pumping into him. He touched the glowing ember to the fuse, and it sputtered into a hissing life of its own. Behind him, Cullison's horse fell, almost invisible under a blanket of scaled, slithering death.

Cullison felt his sight dimming, but he refused to fall until he heard the thunder of the dynamite, and then he sank to his knees and was dragged to the ground by the scaly horde.

A half hour later, a group of three locals were gathered outside Miller's General Store on Casselman's only actual street. "Is that a horse?" said Lem Fuller, the town mayor and magistrate. At the end of the street, a horse slowly staggered into view. As it came closer, Tom Dawson, the farrier said, "Looks like a military saddle on him."

XXVIII

"Looks like he's dragging something on a rope," added Fraser Dunne, "but I can't see what it is; it's a mighty long rope."

The exhausted animal stumbled down the street, and as it came closer, the men could see the froth dripping from its mouth. It took two more steps and collapsed in front of the Paradise Saloon. Fuller and Dawson approached the horse carefully, as if they expected it to jump up and bolt away, refreshed by its brief rest. Fraser Dunne followed the rope to what looked like a bundle of rags fifty feet away.

Dunne realized the weight the horse was dragging was a man, or what was left of him. Scraps of a cavalry uniform hung in tatters from ragged flesh. Dunne nudged the corpse with the toe of his boot, and when it rolled over, he saw the dead soldier's face, blackened where skin still adhered to the skull, and eyes bulging from the sockets. The tongue was little more than shreds of dirt-caked meat where it protruded from torn lips.

Then, a rattlesnake slithered out of the tunic. Dunne froze as the serpent's head turned and its black shining eyes locked on his. The rattler gave him an arrogant flick of its tongue, and slithered away, leaving a curving trail in the dust of the street.

XXIX

Collinsville was, as Cullison had described it, not much more of a town than Casselman, one street lined with ramshackle buildings at either hand, most in disrepair, and some boarded up. Even the telegraph lines sagged like slack muscles. Collinsville was a town that just plain gave up, slowly sinking to the status of a ghost town, like silt settling in a pond.

As the seven of them rode into town, Durken saw birds' nests tucked into the eaves and over the window frames of abandoned businesses, and one building, missing its door, had a full grown sow dozing on its side in the sun in the entrance. He saw no people on the street, but he could feel eyes on them from behind the dusty windows.

The door to the town's one cafe swung inward, and a thick stump of a man ambled out with two others behind him. Unlike the town, he was clean, tidy, and well kept down to the last hair in his thick moustache, the shine on the silver star on his chest, and the well-oiled gleam of the Colt he wore low on his hip. He stepped into the street and held up a hand for the party to halt. His companions waited on the porch of the cafe.

"I'm guessing that's Sheriff Curtis Parker," said McAfee, reining Sweetheart to a stop.

McAfee guessed right. "I'm Curtis Parker, Sheriff of this territory. I take it you're the men I got a telegram about? Here to look into Moses Dutton and his family?"

"If that's the family killed by snakes, then that's who we are." McAfee introduced himself in particular and the rest of the party in general. "If you'd be so good as to give us directions, we'll go take a look at the place."

"I'll do better than that," Parker said, "I'll take you there myself." He turned to the deputies. "Roy, bring my horse around." The taller of the two deputies strolled away, obviously in no hurry. "We've kept the horses inside and the people too. Everybody's pretty spooked."

"How many dead?" said McAfee.

"Four. Mose, his wife Charlotte, and their two sons, Roy and David."

"Best you can tell, when did they die?" said Tate.

"Two days ago. Fellow named Jud Whitson, works as a hand when they need him, saw them all hale and hearty one day, and dead the next."

"Then you got here pretty quick," Durken said.

"Just so happened I was here on my regular rounds. I cover three counties, you know."

Johnny brought Parker's horse, a pinto as short and sturdy as he was, rigged with fancy tack.

Durken said in a low voice to McAfee, "I'd say Parker's "rounds" include more than simple lawman duties to pay for that saddle."

McAfee nodded. "Maybe he's got his fingers in the gambling dens and whorehouses, or some other illegal activity; funny for a man who seems as if he'd never soil his hands with actual dirt."

Parker took the lead as they rode northwest out of Collinsville. "Ten years ago, this town was a thriving enterprise. Miners came from all over and had to live in a tent city because there weren't enough buildings to house them all. Then, like a lot of the towns around here, when the copper ran out, so did the miners. A few stayed on to farm, like Moses Dutton, and some of the shopkeepers stayed around, but most of the people left."

"Have you ever heard of large dens of snakes in the area?" Willoughby said.

Parker shook his head. "Nope. We have our share of rattlers, all kinds; Prairie Rattlers, Hopis, Mojaves, and Sidewinders, but I've never seen more than one at a time."

"How far is the Dutton place from the old copper mine?"

"The Black Horse Mine, four or five miles." Parker pointed west. "The portal lies at the base of that tall mesa you see over that way." In the distance they could see a rough hewn plateau of reddish stone rising from the grassy flatland around it.

"Anybody do any mining there anymore?" Willoughby said, "Digging, blasting, anything that might stir up a nest of snakes?"

Not for a couple of years that I know of," Parker replied. "The entrance is boarded up, but of course, I'm not here every day of the week, so I can't say for sure."

"Ever been in the Dark Horse yourself, Sheriff?" Tate asked.

Parker turned to look Tate in the eye. "I used to be the foreman."

"Then you can be a help to us," said McAfee. I have a feeling we'll be going in it before too long."

The Dutton farm lay at the bottom of a shallow dip in the otherwise level landscape. The men crossed a narrow stream that ran under a small bridge made of rough hewn timber. On the other side, the farmhouse stood to the left in a sparse grove of juniper trees. To the right, they saw a field with the stalks of harvested corn and rows of vegetables tended with great care.

The house itself, a glorified log cabin with a sloping shake roof, was connected to the barn behind it with a sort of cloister made of the same rough lumber as the bridge. As they rode up, a stubbled old man in grey overalls over a Union suit came out of the barn, a shapeless slouch hat riding his ears.

That's Jud Whitson," Parker said. Then in a louder voice, "Ho, Jud."

"Sheriff," Whitson said in a voice that seemed too reedy for his size and age, collapsing the two syllables into "Sherf."

"Everything quiet here?"

"If that's a joke, it ain't funny. Mose and his family been dead for two days and ain't in the ground yet. They deserve a Christian burial."

"Well, you can do for them as soon as these men have a look."

"Have you seen any more snakes?" Willoughby said, dismounting from his horse.

Jud's eyelids closed a little from top and bottom. His jaw thrust forward and he took a long breath. "Is that all you care about? There's four dead here, and they was good people. And you're worrying about snakes?" He took a step toward Willoughby and Parker moved between them.

"Jud, I know you were friends with Mose and his family, but these men need to know what happened here so it won't happen to others."

Jud glared at Willoughby. "Ain't seen no snakes, just dead people. And Toby."

"Toby?" said McAfee.

"The family dog," Parker explained. "A big shepherd."

"But they didn't harm the cows or the pigs." Durken said, pointing to the pen behind the barn where the animals milled around, oblivious to the situation. "What about horses?"

"Nowhere to be seen. I figure they jumped the stile and ran away."

Parker tied his horse to a post in the yard. "Let's show them the bodies, Jud. Get this over with."

The men entered the barn and immediately winced at the smell of putrefaction. Parker lit a cigar. "No disrespect intended," he said when Jud shot him an angry look."To kill the smell."

In the center of the barn floor lay five bodies, each wrapped in a blanket, the smallest one obviously Toby. Tate crouched beside the bodies and peeled away the blanket from the nearest. It was one of the Dutton boys, his tousled sandy hair a stark contrast to his darkened skin. Fang marks · dotted his cheeks and throat.

"That's Roy," said Jud, removing his hat and holding it in both hands.

Willoughby hunkered down beside Tate, waving away the swarm of flies that buzzed around the bodies. He pulled out a small ruler. "All sizes," he said after a minute's measuring. "That likely means all ages."

"Did they all die in the barn?" Tate asked.

"I found Mose and David in the field. Roy was in the barn, and Miz Dutton was in the back yard hanging wash on the clothes line."

"Sounds as if the snakes got them all at the same time," said Durken. "No one was running away. They were all going about their everyday business. It's as if the snakes came from all sides at once and surprised them."

"What about the dog, Toby?" Willoughby said.

Jud pulled the blanket away from the smallest bundle, revealing the black and brown shepherd dog. "He was in the barn with Roy."

Tate had pulled the blanket away from Charlotte Dutton's corpse and began undoing the buttons of her dress.

"What are you doing?" snapped Jud. He grabbed Tate from behind by his coat and yanked him back. He swung Tate in a half circle, throwing him into a stack of hay bales.

Black pulled his pistol, and swung it toward Jud's head. Durken closed his right hand over the revolver so that the flesh between his thumb and forefinger blocked the hammer as it fell. His left hand closed on Black's wrist and he twisted the weapon from his grasp. "No need for that."

"Don't you people have no decency?" shouted Jud.

Tate picked himself up. "Sheriff, we have to examine the bodies and photograph them to compare this to another attack."

"Pitchers?" said Jud. He turned to Parker. "Sheriff, that just ain't right."

"We have to let them do it, Jud. They have Federal authority."

"It ain't right," Jud snarled, and stomped out of the barn.

"Is he a relative?" said McAfee.

"Might as well have been," said Parker. "He's worked for them for years. I understand his feelings."

Durken handed Black his pistol, butt in the air. "Don't be so quick with this." Black glared at him, rubbed his wrist, and said nothing.

Willoughby undid the rest of Charlotte's buttons. Bites pocked the front of the woman's torso from her collarbone to her hips. "Just like the Posset woman," said Willoughby, drawing the blanket over her nakedness. "Ghastly."

A quick examination of the other bodies revealed the same bites and discoloration. "I'll get the camera equipment," said Black.

"We can do that later," said McAfee. "Right now, I want to take a look at the Black Horse Mine." He turned to Parker. "If we go, can you trust Whitson to leave things as they are?"

"I think so." Parker stepped outside the barn with the others behind him. "Jud!"

The hired man came around the corner. "Yeah, Sheriff?"

"We're leaving for a while, but we'll be coming back. I know you want to bury Mose and his family, but I need your word you won't do it before I get back here."

Jud nodded slowly. "I won't bury them, Sheriff. You have my word."

"All right." Then to the others, "Let's saddle up, men."

Jud watched them ride across the bridge, his anger smoldering. "It just ain't right." The family deserved peace and dignity to his reckoning, and he knew what he had to do. Jud went to the shed behind the barn and returned with a five-gallon can of kerosene.

He poured the fuel around the barn, in the hay, and on the blankets over the corpses. He set down the empty can and removed his hat. "Lord, please receive these souls took before their time." He struck a match and watched, tears streaming down his face, as the flames spread. Only when he was sure that the fire took, did Jud walk out of the barn.

A mile from the farm, Parker looked over his shoulder. "Oh, hell."

A column of smoke funneled upward from the barn.

"Well," said Durken, "I guess Jud kept his word. He didn't bury them."

"This is all your fault, McAfee," snapped Tate. "If we'd done what Black and I wanted, we'd have the pictures."

McAfee reined Sweetheart to a stop. "You saw the bodies, Tate. I saw the bodies. We all saw them, and they all look the same as the Possets. You got the testimony of two or three witnesses and then some. I'm more interested in finding those snakes than taking pictures, because if we find the snakes, we'll find who's running them, and maybe find that girl alive. Now let's go."

XXX

Martin and Durst peered over the rocks at the top of the mesa and watched the party approaching from miles away. "They're coming," said Durst.

"Yes," said Martin. "We must tell the Master." They dismounted and tethered their horses. Nearby they found a hole in the red rock that led downward into darkness. The pair climbed into the hole and using handholds cut into the stone years before by the miners, descended into the vent shaft. The further they went, the dimmer the light became, until they were in complete darkness, but their eyes saw as clearly as they would in the full light of day. Their feet touched the floor of the shaft, and the mass of hissing rattlesnakes that covered the rock parted to either side of the passage, opening a path for them to follow.

They moved slowly, but with purpose as the snakes slid aside, following the tunnel to a bend. Beyond it the tunnel dead-ended in a blunt room of rough-hewn rock. Red-skinned men in loincloths, feathers and war paint stood, arms folded, along either side of the chamber. On a throne-like rock, sat a naked, dark skinned, black-haired woman. Martin and Durst approached her and knelt.

From a side chamber, an elderly man appeared. His white hair hung to his shoulders and flowed into the shape of a pebbled cloak of snake skin that hung to the tunnel floor. The shaman said, "Why have you come here?"

"To bring word to you," said Durst in a flat, emotionless voice. "Men come. The men who entered her sanctuary and defiled it."

"See that they die."

"We obey," both said.

"You have done well. Stand now for your reward." The old man began a high-pitched chant. The woman rose from the rock, and as the men watched, her legs twisted and blurred, merging into one sinuous mass as she rose to half again her height. Her skin buttoned out into scales like glittering coins, and her forehead flattened into a reptilian parody of humanity. Her flowing black hair coiled and wound itself into hissing, wriggling serpents, and her eyes turned a glowing yellow, their pupils stretching into black diamonds.

Martin and Durst stepped forward, and the goddess slithered toward them, her elongated arms wrapping around the pair and pulling them to her scaly breasts. Her fanged mouth opened, and its forked tongue flickered around first Durst's face, then Martin's, daubing them with her hypnotic saliva.

Durst gasped in ecstasy, "Thank you, goddess, thank you." Martin was speechless, euphoria overtaking him.

"Now go," hissed the old man, his voice a sibilant rasp. Ki-No-Na-Te released them, and Martin and Durst left the way they came, the snakes closing the path on the floor behind them like rattling water.

Back in the chamber, the cloaked shaman said to his servants, "Bring the child."

Two of the braves left the room for a moment and returned, each one holding an arm of a small girl. Her blonde hair was done in pigtails, one braid coming undone like a frayed rope. Her calico dress was little more than a rag, and her glazed blue eyes stared at nothing.

"Come to me, child."

Eloise Posset stepped forward, eyes-open, sleepwalking. She showed no fear of the snake woman, nor any other emotion, for she was under the goddess's spell. Ki-No Na-Te reached one of her clawed hands out to fondle one of the girl's yellow braids, then curled her fingers around it and pulled the child to her.

Her tongue flicked around the girl's face, painting it with her unholy gift. The child neither flinched nor cried out; she simply sighed, closed her eyes, and turned the corners of her mouth in a beatific smile. Ki-No-Na-Te hissed, then released the girl and nodded to the braves, who took her away.

XXXI

Parker led the riders toward the Black Horse Mine. The mesa was still two miles away, but in the clear air, its red rock was visible in deceptively sharp detail, as if they could reach out and touch it with a

...the goddess slithered towards them...

finger. Beyond the mesa, the sky was darkening and an occasional flash of lightning lit the black thunderheads.

Biggs and Wharton rode behind Parker, with McAfee and Durken following. Willoughby, Tate and Black had dropped back and were engaged in a hushed conversation.

"What do you think they're talking about?" Durken said with a chuckle.

"Probably how to murder us in our sleep," McAfee replied. "I imagine as soon's Tate finds a telegraph, he's going to go moaning to Washington and try to jump our command."

"That's about what I'd expect Tate to do since—" Durken broke off suddenly and reined Thunder to a halt..

"What is it?"

"Top of the mesa, I saw something move."

McAfee shielded his eyes with a hand. "I don't see anything. Maybe it was a pronghorn. There's enough of them around here."

"Too shiny," Durken said, reaching into his saddle bag for his binoculars. He studied the mesa as Tate and his men caught up.

"What's up?" Tate asked.

Durken didn't answer. Parker rode back to them. "Sheriff, you send any of your men out this way?"

Parker shook his head. "Nope. My deputies are back in town. Why?"

"Somebody on that mesa."

"Well," Collins said, "we'll be there in a half hour. If he's still there when we arrive, we'll find out who he is quick enough." He nudged the pinto and rode off.

"He's been out here too long," said McAfee. "Got too comfortable."

"What are you talking about?" said Tate.

"Whoever's on that mesa. Don't want to ride into an ambush," Durken said, taking his rifle from its scabbard and laying it across his saddle. "Out in the open like this, we'd be like tin cans on a fence."

"Ambush? I thought we were looking for snakes."

"We are, but there's too much going on here to let our guard down. I'd'a thought you learned that last time." Durken clucked his tongue and Thunder trotted away before Tate could reply.

XXXII

From the top of the mesa, Durst and Martin watched the riders approach. They were within two hundred yards. Neither spoke. They crouched behind the rocks, each clutching a Winchester, motionless, like machines waiting for someone to pull a lever.

The party below had spread out, putting thirty or forty feet between individual horses. Durst and Martin squinted into the sun. Martin counted eight mounts, including the pack mule.

"Hey boys." They turned slowly and saw McAfee pointing Durken's ten-gauge at them. "Out potting prairie dogs?"

Neither would-be bushwhacker spoke. They stared at McAfee as if waiting for an order. He gave one. "Put the rifles down, fellows, slow and easy. I pull this trigger, you're both gone."

No one moved, then as if one person, Durst and Martin said in one voice, "We obey." They swung their rifles toward McAfee. He pulled both triggers, and the Mackenzie roared. The kick knocked McAfee backward a step and almost put him on his back. He dropped the scatter gun and drew his Colt, but it wasn't necessary. What was left of Martin and Durst was spread across ten feet.

McAfee looked warily around him; satisfied there were no others, he stooped to pick up the Mackenzie. He reloaded it, just in case, sat on one of the rocks that littered the top of the mesa, and rolled a cigarette. He figured he'd let the agents go through the corpses. That was the kind of thing they did best, investigate.

Tate's response to the situation was predictable. "You killed those men before we could question them! What's wrong with you?"

McAfee shook his head. "All I can say, Tate, is that you weren't here. It was them or me. Of course I could've waited 'til they shot a few of you off your horses, but I wasn't going to risk losing Durken. He's too useful."

Enough was left of their faces for Durken to recognize Martin and Durst.

Black knelt at the bodies and gingerly rifled their pockets, coming up with blood soaked papers that confirmed the identification. Bob peered over the edge of the bluff. "There's two horses down below, saddles and gear."

"Theirs, I suppose," said McAfee. "We'll take the bodies back to town.

Ketchum can come claim Martin's if he wants to. That all right with you, Sheriff?"

Parker nodded. "Good for me."

"Ever see these men before, Sheriff?" Tate said.

Parker shook his head. "Can't say I have."

"They were in Portman same day I was," Durken said. "Now they're here. Seems too much of a…what's that word you use, McAfee?"

"Coincidence."

"Yeah that's the word, coincidence."

"You didn't see fit to mention it to me," Tate grumbled.

"Didn't seem important 'til just now."

"Well, if we see Ketchum again, we can tell him what happened to his brother-in-law," McAfee said. "Let's just pile some rocks on them to keep the buzzards and coyotes away. Then, since these boys seem to have wanted to stop us from coming here, we should go into the mine."

"There's an air shaft back there," said Parker, starting across the tabletop. "Used to have an exhaust fan over it, but that's gone now. The hole's boarded up. It's right over this way." He stepped around a boulder and called back, "Here it is, and somebody's uncovered it." The others joined him and stared into the hole. "We'd have to climb down the side on those handholds."

Down the side of the four-foot hole, indentations were cut into the rock. "They were cut to make the airshaft an emergency exit in case of a cave-in."

"How far down?" Durken peered over his shoulder.

"Hundred twenty, hundred thirty feet." He looked at Durken's leg. "It's no easy trip. We might do better going in below."

"Just as well," said McAfee. "I'd hate to run into snakes while we're hanging from our fingernails fifty feet off the floor."

The mine entrance at the foot of the mesa was boarded over with heavy planks and hand-painted signs that warned anyone at large, "keep out" and "danger." The opening was an archway eight feet tall and almost as wide, rounded at the top. Narrow gauge rails ran under the planks like a segmented tongue.

Parker wrapped his hands around one of the planks and tugged at it. It didn't give. He tried a few more. "Doesn't look like anybody's been through here."

"Anybody bring a crowbar?" Tate said. Black snickered.

"This is why we're in charge, not you." Durken took a coil of rope from his saddle. He tied an end around one of the planks and looped the other end around Thunder's saddle horn. "Stand away." He whistled, and the horse trudged forward, tugging at the rope. With a groaning of wood and screech of nails, one end of the plank came loose then swung away, hanging to the side of the tunnel.

Durken patted the horse's side. "Good boy. Couple more and we're done." Shortly, enough of the wood was removed that they could climb through and enter the shaft. They left Biggs and Evans outside as lookouts and lit their lanterns.

Durken and McAfee had been in mine shafts before, and this one looked like most of them. Thick hand-hewn timbers formed arches that propped the ceiling every ten feet or so. The floor was thick with dust and rubble. In the brassy lamplight, the walls, the timbers, the discarded equipment were all the same color from the accumulated grit as if molded from the same pot of clay.

Parker peered around his lantern. "No tracks, here, except four footed varmints, rats and such. He shone his lantern into a straight tunnel that sloped downward into blackness.

"How far does that shaft run?" said Tate.

"Almost a thousand feet at a three percent grade. It splits off into side tunnels along the way." He stepped around an ore car chocked at the top of the slope. They followed Parker single-file beside the tracks, their footsteps echoing down the shaft.

"No way to skulk around in here, is there?" said McAfee.

"Maybe we should've worn moccasins," Durken replied, shining his lantern on the beams overhead. "Parker, how likely is this shaft to cave in?"

"Not likely at all," said the sheriff over his shoulder. "The timbers are solid. They're too new to rot."

"I'll take your word for it." He shined his light on the next set, tracing the beam across the ceiling.

"I thought you were taking his word," said Black.

"Ever see a snake drop out of a tree?"

"Not a rattler," said Willoughby.

"First time for everything."

They went further and Parker suddenly stopped. "What the..." His lantern shone on a mass of earth and stone that blocked the passage ahead. "A cave-in. When did that happen?"

"This is new?" said Tate.

"I guess so. Never saw it before."

"I think we'd better head back to the surface," McAfee said. "We're cornered in here."

"I agree," said Parker, and the party started back up the shaft the way they came. Outside, they found the soldiers and their horses unharmed.

"What's the plan?" Durken asked McAfee.

"We go back to Collinsville and wait for Cullison and his boys. I have to get a message to the General." He turned to Parker. "I saw telegraph wires when we rode into town. Are they useable?"

"Were the last time I needed them," Parker said. "But that was a while ago. George Bratton, the telegraph operator left last year, and nobody's replaced him."

"We'll manage," said Durken, "so long as things are in working order."

"You an operator?"

He nodded. "Learned it in the war."

Lagging behind, out of earshot, Tate said to Black, "When you went over the bodies, did you get any samples?"

Black shook his head. "What little that fool McAfee left of the faces was so covered in blood I couldn't get a trace that was meaningful."

Tate cursed under his breath. "We'll just have to try again next time. Come on. Let's catch up before they get suspicious."

The party was halfway back to Collinsville when Private Biggs called for a halt.

"What's the matter?" Parker said.

"Listen."

A faint rustling in the near distance, growing louder.

"Which way's it coming from?" said Tate.

"No way and every way," said Biggs. "It's all around us."

The horses began to twitch and whinny. A hundred yards away in every direction, the wiry grass was bending in waves no wind ever created, lying down and springing up again, the deadly circle closing on the riders. At fifty yards, they could see first of the snakes.

"We've got to run for it," said Tate.

"Which way?" said Durken. "They've got us surrounded."

The rustling was louder now, augmented by the angry whir of rattles. "They must be ten feet deep," McAfee said. We could never ride through them without us and the horses getting a dozen bites each."

Durken dismounted. "I got an idea if you got the nerve." He pulled the Mackenzie out of its scabbard and checked the breech. "Get ready to ride when I say." He wrapped thunder's reins around his wrist and went onto one knee, wincing at the pain. He held the shotgun horizontal almost to the ground. "Steady now."

Twenty-five yards.

The sibilant sound was like wind in Durken's ears. He saw the mass of snakes, glittering eyes and scales. "Steady."

Biggs screamed. "I ain't waiting."

"Stop, you fool," shouted McAfee, but it was no use. Biggs spurred his horse and tried to ride through the slithering tide, against the wild-eyed animal's wishes. Like waves in the ocean crashing against a rock, masses of the snakes rose against him and the horse climbing over each other to get to their prey. In seconds, horse and rider disappeared under a blanket of diamond backed horrors.

Fifteen yards.

"Get ready, boys. This is it." Durken took a deep breath. Thunder pawed the ground nervously, the other frightened mounts almost dancing in their desire to escape.

Five yards.

Durken pulled the first trigger. The double-aught buckshot cut a five-foot swath through the grass, blowing the snakes apart. "Go!" He pulled the second trigger and widened the path through the closing circle. The riders took off. Not even the pack mule balked at the flight. Durken put his foot in the stirrup. "Hut!" he shouted at Thunder. The bay needed no second urging; he took off at a full gallop, Durken hanging from his side and gripping the saddle horn.

The gap in the snakes closed rapidly, and Durken barely made it through. One snake struck at him and grazed his boot in the stirrup. Another buried its fangs in his chaps, stopped by the patch of buffalo hide.

A hundred yards from the snakes, Durken called out, "Ho!" and Thunder stopped abruptly. Durken jumped from the stirrup and pulled his Bowie knife from the sheath. One quick swipe severed the wriggling rattler's head from its body, and he leaned against Thunder, half swooning from the pain in his leg and the shock of the ordeal.

McAfee rode up beside him as the others continued their flight. "You all right?"

"Yeah, but that was way too close." He poked the point of the knife between the fangs of the snake head and pried it from his chaps.

"Well, you better saddle up. Looks as if the snakes ain't done with us yet." McAfee pointed back the way they came, and they could see the grass, this time all moving in one direction.

They caught up to Parker and the others. "They're still after us." The sheriff said, looking back over his shoulder. "What do we do?"

"We could outrun them, but where do we go?" McAfee said. "If we go back to town and they follow us there, they'll kill everything in the place."

Willoughby spoke up. "Sheriff, when's the last time it rained here?"

"Maybe a week ago, but not much."

Willoughby wet a finger and held it to the wind. "Wind's coming from our right. Let's head into it and see if the snakes follow."

"What about Biggs?" said Evans.

"He'll still be there when we're done," Durken said, "If we live through this."

The party headed north into the wind, riding more slowly to keep the pursuing snakes in sight. "How far are we from Collinsville, Sheriff?" Willoughby asked.

"A good eight miles."

"That's far enough. We won't endanger the town." He dismounted and pulled a handful of the wiry buffalo grass from the ground. He rubbed it between his fingers and nodded, satisfied. Willoughby took the lanterns from the pack mule and passed them out to the men. "Spread out, and pour the kerosene from the lanterns on the ground. We're going to start a prairie fire." He looked over his shoulder at the coming storm. "And hope the rain doesn't start any too soon."

Following Willoughby's lead, the men poured kerosene on the grass in a curving line a hundred yards across so that the wind would push it inward. They waited for his signal to light it. "Not 'til you see the whites of their eyes, gentlemen." The rushing sound came closer, and the grass bent under the weight of the attackers. Behind them, the wind picked up and Durken could smell the approaching rain. Fifty yards. Willoughby tested the wind with his finger again and said simply, "Now."

The men struck matches and set the grass aflame. Soon, an unbroken line of orange fire raged over a hundred yards. Spurred by the wind, the fire line belled outward in a blazing crescent that swept across the flatland toward the onrushing snakes.

Thunder cracked behind the men and the first drops of rain began to fall. They stood steady, holding their horses' reins to keep them from bolting. There is a reason that animals instinctively fear fire, that creatures in a burning forest, natural enemies, predators and prey, will run as one to flee its all-devouring power. The snakes defied the biological imperative.

The serpents and the flames flowed toward each other like a pair of clashing armies. Parker peered through the billowing smoke. "They aren't turning, Willoughby," he said. "They're running right into it."

"I was hoping to trap them before they could get away and then kill as many as possible. I didn't expect mass suicide."

"They're on a mission." said Durken.

The wall of flame surged into the mass of snakes. Some broke through, charred and smoking, only to writhe and bite at themselves in agony in the brittle, blackened grass. The scent of burnt meat was strong enough that even the roiling black smoke from the fire couldn't mask it.

The storm broke and pelted the party and their horses with rain like buckshot. In minutes, they were soaked to the skin, and the fire was all but extinguished, but it was too late to save the snakes. When the rain quit, Black set up his camera and photographed the grisly scene

The men stood at the ready to kill anything that crossed the strip of blackened grass, but few even made the attempt. An hour later, after the fire was out, the men picked their way across the steaming black ground among the bodies of hundreds of snakes.

Willoughby lifted one from the ground with his stick. "They all seem to be rattlers. Whoever's controlling these snakes is particular. I'm glad it's just the rattlers. Imagine what we'd have if all the species were in play."

"That's a sobering thought," said Tate.

"But at the same time, that may be useful. Rattlers have a natural enemy. King snakes eat them."

"Where are we going to find enough king snakes to manage a horde this size?"

Willoughby shook his head. "We aren't. What we need to do is find who's behind this and stop him."

"Or her," Durken added.

"Her?"

"Ki-No- Na-Te, the Snake Mother."

In the bowels of the earth, the goddess twitched like a spider that feels a tug at its web. The serpents that wreathed her head twisted in angry knots. The defilers dared enter her sacred places, speak her name. The shaman's hands closed into bony fists. Today's children were dead, but he would call more, many more to her and make all of the defilers pay with their lives.

XXXIII

The telegraph office in Collinsville was dusty from disuse, but the equipment was in good repair, unlike most of the town. "What do we tell the General?" he asked McAfee.

"Tell him where we are. Tell him we had a confrontation and we'll send a report by courier. I don't want to send details over the wire. Too many words, too many ears. We can get Evans to ride with it. I'm sure he'll be glad to be shut of this place. Or maybe he can hand it off to one of Cullison's men in Casselman."

Durken tapped the telegraph key and waited for a response. In a moment, the key rattled as another operator acknowledged their signal. "Line's working."

"Send the message to the General in Bacon Rock. I hope he's still there."

"Wait a minute." The telegraph key chattered. "Message coming in for the sheriff. Oh, hell."

They listened to the clacking key as it spelled out a message for Sheriff Parker: CASSELMAN STOP COME AT ONCE STOP SOLDIERS DEAD STOP

Durken tapped the code for receipt of the message and stared for a moment at the now silent key. "This is more than we thought, maybe more than the General thought."

"But it isn't more than Tate thought. Did you notice that he and Black didn't seem surprised today when the snakes came after us?"

"Now that you mention it, neither one looked very surprised at anything. Black took his photographs like they were pictures of a picnic."

"I think it's time we sat those two down and had a long talk."

"First, I have to send the message to the General." He tapped in dot-dot-dot-dash-dash, dash-dash-dash-dash-dot. The number thirty-nine, telegrapher's code: IMPORTANT WITH PRIORITY ON THROUGH WIRE. The telegraph rattled in response: dot-dash-dash-dash-dash. Thirteen: I UNDERSTAND. A second response, and a third, then silence. The line was cleared.

He named General Sherman as the recipient and Bacon Rock as the destination. The message McAfee dictated was simple: NEW INCIDENTS CASSELMAN AND COLLINSVILLE STOP WILL SEND WRITTEN REPORT STOP DURKEN AND MCAFEE.

"You figure the General knows about Casselman already?"

"Could be, but we'd better fill him in as soon as we can. Get Tate to write it up. That'll keep him busy, and we can take a look at it before we send it out. Make sure he isn't stacking the deck for Washington."

"But send it to the General and nobody else."

Durken nodded agreement. "Yeah, the Secret Service can wait. Speaking of waiting, I'll stick around to see if we get a reply."

"I'll go find Parker and see what he wants to do about Durst and Martin."

"I'd be inclined to leave them for the buzzards."

"No argument there, but we're going to have to go back to the Black Horse Mine anyway."

"You go ahead and find Parker. I'll wait to hear from the General. While I wait, I'll get a message off to Sheriff Bennet back in Bacon Rock; send word about Martin and Durst in case Ketchum comes back. And while you're out looking, go find a bottle of whiskey. My flask ran dry, and I could use a drink"

"You and me both." McAfee left the telegraph office and paused for a moment looking up and down the dusty street. Nothing moved in the red light of sunset, as if the town were holding its breath, waiting to see what would happen next.

McAfee pushed apart the swinging doors of the Copper Queen, Collinsville's only operating saloon. It had the look of once being prosperous, but like the rest of the town, it had fallen to dust and disrepair. Spidery cracks ran from a corner of the mirror behind the bar halfway across its glass. Cobwebs adorned an upright piano, and the floor looked as if it hadn't seen a broom in a year. Behind the bar, a crook-backed man in overalls and a flannel shirt leaned against it looking half asleep.

He found Willoughby at a table away from the doors. "Where's Tate?"

"He's with the sheriff," Willoughby said.

"No surprise there. I'm sure they have a lot to talk about. And Black?"

"He's down the street working with the pictures he took today."

McAfee went to the bar and came back with a glass and a bottle. "So, Willoughby," he said, "what can you tell me about today I don't already know?"

Willoughby looked to McAfee's bottle and his empty glass. McAfee poured him a drink and he downed half of it before he spoke. "What we saw today defies all logic. Snakes shy away from fire instinctively, as do all animals, but for some reason those rattlers were so hell bent on chasing us that the fire didn't even slow them down. They showed no sense of self-preservation whatsoever. Ever hear of lemmings?"

McAfee nodded. "I read about them in some book once. Little critters that follow each other off of cliffs and kill themselves for no reason?"

Willoughby nodded. "It's not quite that simple, but close enough. These snakes exhibited the same type of suicidal behavior. That and attacking like a coordinated army; it baffles me."

"Now tell me something I don't know about Tate and Black and the Secret Service."

"You heard Tate. Washington sees the situation as a 'threat to national security.' Imagine a tide of snakes swarming through the Capitol while Congress in session."

"That Parliament of whores? I'd say it'd be a case of 'hail, fellow, well met.'" McAfee laughed in spite of himself and so did Willoughby. McAfee downed his drink and poured another. He stared across the table at Willoughby, serious now and said, "There's things about this business Tate knows and we don't. You may not know all of them, but I figure you must know some. It's time you told me. Durken and I are tired of stumbling around in the dark."

"I'll tell you what I know, which isn't much. Tate's reckless. We would've been killed today with him in charge. I'll put my money for staying alive on you two." The stub in his pipe had gone out. He scratched a match on the table and in a minute, his head was wreathed in smoke. "I don't suppose Tate told you there were other attacks."

"Others? How many others?"

"Two that I know of, but Tate doesn't tell me everything, either."

"Where did they happen?"

"Within twenty miles or so of here. Both were out in nowhere land."

"So this isn't happening all over the territory. What we're seeing is all in one area, more or less."

"More or less."

"How long ago?"

"It's hard to tell because they weren't found right away; six or eight weeks, give or take."

"Does Parker know this?"

Willoughby looked away. "The other attacks happened outside his jurisdiction, and Tate didn't think we needed to tell him."

McAfee didn't speak for a while. He swirled the whiskey in his glass. "We killed all those snakes today, Willoughby, but we're not done by a stretch."

"What do you mean?"

McAfee told Willoughby about Cullison and his men. "Unless those snakes flew here from Casselman after they killed the soldiers, we're dealing with a whole different pack of them. We have to find out who's behind this...or what, and deal with it. That business Durken brought up, the Snake Mother, I'm not superstitious, but Durken and I've seen some things in our time riding together that, like you say, defy logic. "

"Have you told Parker or Tate about what happened in Casselman?"

McAfee shook his head. "Ain't seen either one to tell them yet, but I'll have to. Like it or not, we need them, and the deputies if we're going into that mine."

"And we'll have to do it."

"No other way."

XXXIV

Tate looked over his shoulder and saw no one on the street as he slipped into the darkened telegraph office. In the twilight through the dusty front window, he saw the table with the operator's rig. He struck a match and saw that the wires were attached to the rig. The telegraph was hooked up, Durken's doing, no doubt. He sat in the chair and tapped the key. In a moment it chattered in response. Tate smiled. This was going better than he'd hoped.

Tate cleared the line and quickly sent a message: COLLINSVILLE STOP CLOSING ON OBJECT STOP ALERT FLINTLOCK STOP REPLY STOP ARROWHEAD.

He waited thirty seconds, a minute, two. No response. He tapped the key again: REPLY.

"They can't reply to something you never sent," Durken said, stepping from the darkness of the next room, holding a pair of wires in his left hand and his right dangling over his Colt. "Now suppose you tell me who this Flintlock fellow is."

XXXV

"The fellow who gives Tate his orders is Arhur McMonagle." Willoughby poured another glass of whiskey. "I've heard Tate and Black refer to him by the nickname Flintlock. He's the Secret Service's Assistant Deputy Chief. "

"Sounds about right," McAfee said. "Put a fancy title on a man, and he thinks the rules aren't for him anymore. Why're Durken and I even here if they don't want us to know what's what?"

"Sherman apparently is the top dog in these parts because of the Indian situation; that and his relationship with President Grant. The last time Tate came out here, Sherman raised such hell all the way to Washington that they didn't dare come nosing around again unannounced. Tate pitched a holy fit when he found out that not only were you and your partner coming along on this expedition, but you'd be in charge as well."

Parker came into the saloon with his deputies in tow. McAfee jerked his head toward the new arrivals. "And Parker? What's gone between him and Tate?"

Willoughby shrugged. "You'll have to ask him. Tate seems to operate by giving everyone involved part of the picture and never letting anybody look at the whole thing. From what I've seen of Parker, I'd say he's out for himself first, second, and third."

"I'd agree."

Parker nodded to the bartender and walked behind the bar. He took a glass for himself from a shelf under the counter and headed for the table. His deputies slouched at the bar waiting for the bartender to pour their whiskeys.

Parker hooked a chair away from the table with his foot and sat. He pointed to the bottle and raised his eyebrows. "Help yourself," McAfee said. "Just leave some for Durken."

Parker poured himself a healthy slug. "Hell of a thing today." He leaned forward, elbows on the table and hands cradling his glass. "Those people at the farm, that soldier." Parker shuddered. "Dreadful."

"Turns out that's not all." McAfee handed the sheriff the telegram from Casselman. Parker read the message and the lines in his face deepened. "Did Tate happen to tell you there were two other attacks in the last six weeks?"

Parker's head snapped up. "What? Two more where?"

"East of here," said Willoughby.

"Tate knew that? Why didn't he tell me?"

"Same reason he didn't tell us," McAfee said. "He's playing this game close to his vest, and it's time we found out about it."

The doors to the Copper Queen swung inward and Tate walked in followed by Durken. Three steps into the saloon the men at the table saw that Durken had his Colt pointed at Tate's back and held Tate's revolver in his other hand. "Caught him sending a message to his bosses in Washington on the telegraph. I pulled the wires before it went through, but I heard the message. Something about 'closing on the object.'"

Tate's face was expressionless but his eyes darted around the room like a trapped animal. McAfee kicked a chair out. "Have a seat, Tate. You have some explaining to do." Parker's deputies straightened up. They edged away from the bar and away from each other, spreading out. Parker put up a hand to hold them back.

Tate hesitated and Durken put his pistol behind Tate's ear and cocked the hammer. "Do what you're told."

"You won't shoot," Tate said, looking straight ahead.

Durken pulled the trigger and the Colt boomed next to Tate's ear.

"Oh, Jesus!" Tate clapped his right hand to the side of his head. Durken moved the pistol to the other side of the agent's head and cocked it again. "Now what?"

"All right. All right," Tate said, and sat in the chair.

"Start talking, Tate," McAfee ordered, "and don't stop 'til you tell us everything you know about all this."

XXXVI

Miles away, a dark figure rode toward Casselman astride a dappled grey stallion. He wore the severe black garb of a minister and held the horse's reins in his right hand and a well-used Bible in his left. From beneath his flat brimmed hat white hair cascaded, dancing in the wind, and a pair of eyebrows curved like iron wings above his blazing green eyes. Behind him rode a rag-tag coterie of men and women, coincidentally twelve in number. Their faces were gaunt and grim, testimony to a life of self-denial.

None spoke until the faint glow of the town's lights came into view. The man riding right behind the minister broke the silence. "Pastor Bungard," he said. "What is this place?"

"It is the place where we will confront the evil and destroy it, Caleb. The nest of the Serpent. The spirit told me so."

Murmurs of "Amen" and "Praise the Lord," ran through the flock, and once more, the only sound was the horses' hooves on the hardscrabble road.

Durken pulled the trigger…

XXXVII

"**Y**ou two don't know what a tall ledge you're jumping off." Tate spoke as if he were talking about the weather. "I'm a Federal agent." Durken still pointed his pistol at Tate's head.

"And in a manner of speaking, so are we," McAfee responded. "And at the moment, we're a rung higher than you on that ladder. Since I'm the one giving orders, I'm ordering you to tell us what you're holding back about this business. Start with the two attacks before Casselman."

Tate's eyes darted to Willoughby, who shrugged.

"We were damn near killed today," he said, looking at Tate over the rims of his eyeglasses. "Twice. These two," he nodded toward Durken and McAfee, "pulled us out of the jaws both times. I figure the more they know, the safer we'll all be. I was you, I'd tell them."

Tate looked to Parker. "Sheriff, you can't just let these men…"

"I agree with Willoughby, Tate," Parker said. "And I agree with McAfee too; we can't go at this problem with one eye shut."

Seeing no sympathy in the room, Tate took a deep breath and started to talk.

"After the incident with the Cat Warriors, my superior…"

"That would be McMonagle," said McAfee.

"Flintlock," Durken added.

"Yes. McMonagle thought it was worthwhile to put me in charge of a special division of the Service, one to look into things that aren't natural or normal. Now, it's my job and Black's to investigate these incidents, determine whether they pose a threat to the country, and gather as much information about them as I can."

"So the Secret Service could use these things as weapons," said McAfee. "Just like you wanted to learn how to convert men into monsters like the Cat Warriors, make a whole army of them if you want to."

"Never mind the why; think about the how. The how is out there. Would you rather Mexico get it first? Or Maybe England, so they can use it to take us back as a colony. Or maybe somebody like Napoleon to conquer Europe. Don't you see? If we get it first, we learn to control it, and nobody can use it against us."

"And we all know the motives of the Secret Service are virgin pure," McAfee said, rolling his eyes.

Tate ignored him and went on. "We have to learn the how before other people do."

"And who are these other people?" asked Durken. "I don't see no Chinamen or A-rabs sneaking around here."

"That's the whole point, damn it. It could be an agent from any government. They'd all be eager as a dog in heat to get their hands on the secret, and they will be as soon as they know it's out there. If they don't already know."

McAfee held up a hand. "You still haven't told us what we don't know about the snakes, just a lot of fol-de-rol sounds like some politician making a speech. Now get to it, Tate. Tell us about the other attacks."

"All right. Put down your gun. Let him go."

Black stood just inside the doors of the Copper Queen, aiming a Winchester at Durken, who turned his head to look in the spidered mirror over the bar. "I got good eyes, Black. Even from this far I can see that rifle ain't cocked, 'cause you didn't want to make any noise. You think you can lever a shell into the chamber and pull the trigger before any or all of us," he cocked his head toward McAfee and Parker, "can pull and shoot you dead? Besides that," he swung his pistol toward Black and cocked the hammer, "mine's already out the holster."

"Put the gun down, Black," Tate said, staring straight ahead, still speaking in the same matter-of-fact voice.

"But they're…"

"Don't be stupid, Black. Trust me; they'll kill you and not even blink. Put down the gun. Now!"

Black reluctantly lowered the rifle. One of Parker's deputies stepped over and took it from him by the barrel.

"Pull up a chair, Black," said Parker. "We're having a pow-wow. You might as well join the conversation."

Black sat across the table from Tate.

"Pistol on the table. Hands too," said McAfee. "Don't want you pulling some Derringer out of your vest or your boot."

Black glared at McAfee. "You have no idea what you're getting yourself into."

"Heard that speech already from Tate." He turned to the agent. "Now, you were about to tell us about the other attacks."

"They were both in remote locations, away from even the smallest towns, and they weren't discovered right away, so it's not sure which one was first. One was a prospector named Harshaw found in a shack by one of his friends passing by. The other was a Cavalry patrol out toward Ames. In both cases, there were dozens of bites on the bodies, animals too."

McAfee turned to Parker. "Sheriff, you got a map of the territory handy?"

"I'm sure we can find one." He took a ring of keys from his pocket, isolated an iron skeleton key, and handed it to one of his deputies. "Bob, go over to the Black Horse office and bring back that big map's hanging on the wall."

McAfee turned his attention back to Tate. "Six to eight weeks. How have these attacks been kept quiet all this time?"

Tate shrugged. "They were in remote areas. The patrol was kept quiet as a matter of policy. We isolated the people who found Harshaw as soon as we got word, so they didn't have a chance to talk much."

"Isolated?" said Durken. "You mean locked them up?"

"What would you suggest? Take out an ad in the newspapers? Put up some handbills? We're trying to prevent panic by handling the problem quietly. There have been rumors enough already, but we've scotched them."

"How's that? With friendly persuasion?" Durken grunted. "This doesn't sound like the country I served for four years in the war."

"You realize, Tate," Parker said, "that by keeping us in the dark, you put all our lives in danger, not to mention every person lives around here. They need to be told to protect themselves."

"Protect how? You saw what happened today. We were lucky. It was more than even Black and I expected. The only hope is to find the source and stop it before it gets worse."

"Then maybe get the townspeople out of here while they're still alive, before the snakes regroup and attack the town."

"We still have to find the source and destroy it, or it'll just be another town or another family somewhere else."

"That's true, Tate, but I'd rather not have this town in the back of my mind while we're hunting. They're still my first priority."

"You talk about the source," said McAfee. "What's that mean?"

"And the 'object,'" Durken chimed in. "What's that?"

"Sherman told you about the Tonapa?"

"Snake worshippers. Yeah, he told us there were rumors they were back in business."

"It's more than a rumor." Tate turned to look McAfee in the eye. "They have followers, they have a shaman, and they have a goddess. She is the object."

Bob came into the saloon with a map rolled up under one arm. He handed it to Parker, who spread it on the table.

"Now, Tate," said McAfee, "show us where the other attacks happened."

Tate studied the map for a moment. "Here." He put a finger on the map. "And here." McAfee reached in his pocket and pulled out a handful of coins. He put a penny on each location then put a coin on the spot marking Casselman and the one marking Collinsville.

"Judging by the scale of this map, we're looking at a twenty-mile radius, give or take. Somewhere inside that circle…Parker, you know the mines around here. They wouldn't hole up in a working shaft with people coming and going. Where are the played out mines inside that radius?"

"Now that you mention it, there's only one, and it's here." He put a finger on a dot marking a town called Mannville."

"I say that's where we look next." McAfee put a penny on Mannville.

"Like coppering the Queen," Parker said.

"What?"

"Ever play faro?"

McAfee said, "I stick to poker."

"Coppering the queen is putting a penny on the Queen in the layout and betting it will come up on the first draw, or you lose."

"Seems to catch the spirit of things. But before we go to Manville, we have to go in the Black Horse Mine."

"I'm guessing we'll find it cleared out," said Durken.

"Doesn't matter. We still have to check it out. Then we go to Mannville."

"Sheriff!" A deep, resonant voice boomed from the doorway.

The men turned to see the head and shoulders of a white-haired man in black with bushy eyebrows and a flat brimmed hat showing over the saloon doors.

"I'm Sheriff Parker. Who are you, and why are you hiding out there?"

"I am Pastor Saylor Bungard, a man of God, and I will not enter a house of sin."

"Says you. Show me your hands."

The pastor held his hands head high, palms forward. One was empty and one clutched a Bible. "I come armed only with the word of the Lord. I need to talk with you, Sheriff."

"You're doing fine so far."

"The work of the Lord is not for the ears of run-of-the-mill sinners."

Parker sighed. "All right, Reverend, I'll come out. Roy, come along." The deputy stood, hand over his holster and followed Parker outside.

"What the hell's going on now?" said Durken.

"I can tell you," said Willoughby, "but you won't much like it. The Right Reverend Saylor Bungard is the Pastor of the Pillar of Fire Salvation

Church of Bitter Creek, Nebraska. He and his pack of loonies followed us all around the state when I was with the Magnus Medicine Show. They handle snakes as part of their religious services, quoting Jesus when he says the righteous won't be bitten.

"He said we were disciples of the Antichrist because we handled snakes but we were doing it for Mammon not the Lord." Willoughby shook his head. "More the like, he was worried we were stealing his thunder."

"Think it's a coincidence him showing up here?" McAfee scratched a match on the table and lit a cigarette.

"Not likely," Willoughby replied. "He's a spooky one. Once, a sidewinder got out of the pen in the middle of a crowd at the show. I'd milked him an hour before, and he couldn't have done much harm, but the crowd fell into a panic. Before I could grab him, Bungard stepped out of the mob, and he pointed his finger at the snake. His eyes rolled back in his head, and he started talking a lot of gibberish."

"You mean like speaking in tongues?" Durken said. "I saw that once when I was a boy. No snakes, though."

"Yeah, that's what folks said it was, and I'll be damned if that sidewinder didn't go limp like he was knocked out. Bungard picked up that snake and held it over his head and shouted 'It is the brazen serpent in the wilderness! Look upon it and live, ye sinners.' He strutted off with that snake in the air, and the whole crowd followed him. Damndest thing I ever saw. That night we left Nebraska and never went back."

"And now he's here."

Willoughby nodded in resignation. "And now he's here."

"You're awful quiet, Tate," Durken said. "Nothing to say about this turn of events?"

Tate didn't speak, didn't move, didn't blink.

"You invited Bungard here, didn't you?"

Tate looked straight ahead. "In dire situations, you use every tool in the box until you find one that works."

"That's a good word for how you see us all."

Tate was about to reply when Parker came back in shaking his head. "He wants to take on the snakes with his Bible. Either that man's crazy as a loon, or he's a saint."

"Maybe he's a 'Knight of Faith,'" McAfee said.

Tate smiled. "Kierkegaard, *Fear and Trembling*. McAfee, you never cease to surprise me."

"Saint, loon, or both, we have to deal with him." Durken ground out his cigarette on the table. "So, Tate, tell us exactly what you had in mind when you invited him to this square dance."

"Simple, really," the agent said. "Fight fire with fire. The Patapa are a cult. Fight religion with religion. Willoughby's seen him control snakes before."

"That was one snake," said McAfee, "and a milked one at that, not a couple of hundred ready to bite."

"I'm willing to let him try."

"I'm not," said Durken. He looked to McAfee. "You?"

"Been enough people killed already."

"Maybe you should talk to the Pastor," said Tate, "See what he has to say."

"You called him here, Tate" said McAfee. "You send him home."

XXXVIII

McAfee and Durken took the first room at the top of the stairs over the Copper Queen. Willoughby and Evans took the next room, and Tate and Black had the one on the other side at the back of the building. "Glad to have a room between us and the agents," Durken said, lighting the miner's lantern hanging by a hook beside the door. The lens focused the light in a three foot circle on the opposing wall and lit the room enough to read the headline of a newspaper but not the small print.

"I agree. Hate to think how tired they'd be in the morning from taking turns standing with an ear to the wall all night. Wouldn't be worth much."

"Hell, they're less than worthless now, working contrary to us."

"Tate seems to have strings leading in every direction. Think that preacher's the real deal, or do you think he's a fake?"

Durken pulled off a boot and shook grit from it onto the floor. "Dunno." He pulled off his other boot and held onto it for a minute, thinking. "Question seems to be whether Tate thinks he's a fake. Willoughby seems to think there's something to him."

"But Willoughby works for Tate."

"Yep. That does drop him a rung on the trust ladder. You read Black's report?"

"It's accurate as far as it goes; I added a few bits and pieces he left out. I'll give it to Evans in the morning. You think Tate'll try to send another telegram?"

"First chance he gets, but it won't be from here; not unless he's got a spare battery in his saddlebags. I hid the one from the office." Durken shook out his other boot and set the pair beside his bed. He crossed the room and tilted its one ladder-backed chair against the door.

"Chair's too tall to put under the knob to jam it," McAfee said. "What good'll that do?"

"Lets us both sleep instead of one of us awake on watch. Door opens out. Somebody jiggers the lock and opens it, the chair falls and makes a racket and wakes us up. Now he's got something to step over. While he manages that for half a second, we shoot him."

McAfee stared at Durken. "You think that up all by yourself?"

Durken nodded. "I have my moments."

"Glad we're sleeping in the same room."

Durken shucked off his trousers and opened the slit cut in his Union suit. The stitches that closed his wound were scabbed over, and the skin around them still burned an angry red. Durken opened the tin of Charlie's salve and rubbed it into the skin. The wound hurt once in a while now instead of constantly, but when it did it still got his attention.

"How's it healing?"

"It quit bleeding three days ago, but it's still weeping a little from infection."

"I'd bet on Charlie's medicine. He knows more than we ever will."

"About that, yeah, I'd say he does."

"Better turn out that light. Morning won't arrive any slower if it's on."

"Looks like a train coming."

McAfee turned down the wick and the room went dark. And each left the other to his thoughts until both were sound asleep.

Down the hall, Tate was talking quietly to Black. "Next time you think you're going to rescue me from those two, don't."

Black's face flushed. "I had the drop on Durken."

"He'd've shot you, me, and the Four Horsemen of the Apocalypse before you got the hammer back. Don't you understand? We can't deal with those two on their terms. Maybe we could buffalo that sheriff and his men, but not Durken and McAfee." He stood and headed for the door.

"Where are you going?"

"I have to meet with Bungard and tell him what's what. If I don't set him straight from the jump, who knows what he might say or do. Crazy bastard."

"Want me to go with you?"

"No, I want you to stay here and keep your ears open. If you hear McAfee and Durken leave their room, follow them and see what they're up to."

Black nodded, and Tate with a practiced stealth, slipped out the door and down the hallway, making no sound. He stood outside the cowboys' room for a moment, listening to snores and heavy breathing. Satisfied they were asleep, Tate walked down the staircase, across the darkened saloon, and through the swinging doors into the night.

The town was quiet. Too quiet for Tate's liking. There should have been a dog barking, a cat yowling, or maybe some drunk singing "Sweet Betsy From Pike" to the three-quarter moon that looked like a face just turning to glance his way, but there was no sound. Further up the street he heard it, the monotone recitation of the 23rd Psalm. "'Yea, though I walk through the valley of the shadow of Death, I will fear no evil . . .'"

A few more steps brought Tate to the entrance of an abandoned dry goods store where the light of a candle flickered within. Tate stepped inside and found Saylor Bungard's flock in various sleeping poses huddled on the bare floor while he stood in their midst reciting scripture as if it flowed directly from the closed Bible clenched in his fist to his vocal cords.

"Looks as if you put your flock to sleep, Bungard."

The pastor turned and studied Tate as if he'd never seen him before. "Like the Garden of Gethsemane, Agent Tate. The Lord prayed the night through, and one by one his apostles fell to the weariness of the flesh. Yet they were men of faith, one and all."

"Just as well they're asleep. We need to talk."

"Then talk." Bungard sat on an empty crate. "Speak in the tongues of men, but remember that without love, your words are a noisy gong or a clashing cymbal. What do you love, Agent Tate?"

The question threw Tate. He stammered first then said, "I love my country and hate any enemy that threatens it. But I'm not here to talk about me. What about you? Are you ready to serve your country?"

Bungard turned his Bible over in his hands, reflecting before he answered. "The Savior tells us, 'Render Caesar's things unto Caesar, but God's things unto God.' Sometimes, a man of faith can do both at one stroke. Defeating the Adversary and his minions serves the Lord. If the United States of America may benefit, it is no sin."

"You'll have your chance to serve both if you do what I tell you. There is a town a day's ride from here. Its name is Mannville. There you will find a copper mine, and there you find your Adversary, but you must leave after I have gone with the others in the morning and tell no one. They would stop you if they knew and keep you from your calling. Chain the serpent with the Word of God so that we can throw her into the Abyss for a thousand years."

Bungard's eyes glowed in the dancing candlelight, and he clutched his Bible to his heart. "Faith will triumph! His will be done!"

Tate nodded and strode out of the storefront muttering under his breath, "And the President's."

Back in their room, Black said, "Well?"

"Bungard's on his way, as soon as we leave for the Black Horse Mine. All I had to do was aim him in the right direction."

"What if she's not there?"

"No harm. We'll just keep looking."

"And if she is?"

"Who knows? Maybe his mumbo-jumbo will work."

"What if it works too well and he kills her?"

"He won't. I told him we're going to chain her for a thousand years, right out of Revelation. Bungard's a believer. He won't buck the Bible."

"What if it doesn't work and she kills him?"

"Do you really care?"

Black thought a minute and shrugged. "I guess not. What's Flintlock's word? Expendable?"

"That's the word."

XXXIX

The morning sky was grey, and heavy clouds hung low to the east.

"Smells like rain," Durken said.

"Yep." McAfee threw his saddle over Sweetheart's back and reached under to cinch the girth. "Gonna be a wet day."

"At least it won't be raining in the Black Horse."

"Small comfort, that."

"Tate's up to something." Durken slid his Winchester into the scabbard. "He and Black are in too good a mood for the dressing down they got from us last night."

"I'm not too happy having either one along on this ride. I'd rather Parker locked them up."

"Me too, but we need their eyes and their guns."

"In this situation, can't have too many. Evans!" The private looked as if he hadn't slept. "Are you ready to leave?"

He nodded. McAfee handed him an oilskin packet. "Get this to General Sherman as quick's you can."

"Yes, sir." Without another word, Evans swung into his saddle, kneed his horse in the ribs, and rode out of the corral and down the empty street.

"He's happy to be shut of this place," said Durken.

"Can't say I blame him. I would too."

"Duty."

"Yep."

The group rode out, seven in all, including Willoughby, Tate, and Black, plus Parker and Bob the deputy. As they passed the dry goods store on their way out of town, thirteen pairs of eyes watched from behind the dusty glass. When the horsemen were all but out of sight, Bungard raised his Bible and said, "It is time to face the Adversary!" He looked heavenward and closed his eyes, reciting the scripture as if it were written on the inside of his eyelids.

"'Wherefore take unto you the whole armor of God, that ye may be able to withstand in the evil day, having your loins girt about with truth, and having on the breastplate of righteousness; and your feet shod with the preparation of the gospel of peace; above all, taking the shield of faith, wherewith ye shall be able to quench all the fiery darts of the wicked. And take the helmet of salvation,'"

He held his Bible out in front of him with both hands. "'And the sword of the Spirit, which is the word of God.' Thus saith the Lord."

"Amen. Amen." The murmured word traveled among the flock like echoes in a canyon. They pressed forward, reaching to lay hands upon the Bible. Bungard carefully placed his hat on his head and strode defiantly through the door into the street, his apostles filing out behind him.

XL

McAfee dropped back alongside Tate and Black. "How did the Pastor take the news that he isn't coming along?"

"He was none too happy about it, but he and his people are likely in the saddle by now, going their own way."

"That Bungard looks like a firebrand. Did he succumb to your natural charm, Tate, or did you have to flash your badge at him?"

"Threat of incarceration is a potent incentive."

"For some people." McAfee flicked his reins and Sweetheart picked up his gait to rejoin Durken and Parker in the lead.

Black waited until McAfee was out of earshot. "What'll you do when he finds out you sent Bungard to Mannville?"

"If we're lucky, Bungard will succeed and we come out of this as the heroes who solved the problem. If not…" Tate shrugged. "Ulysses S. Grant still trumps William Tecumseh Sherman."

They saw the carrion birds wheeling in dark circles in the sky before they saw the blackened grass of yesterday's fire.

"Those birds'll have a feast for a day or two, all those snakes," said Willoughby.

"Won't kill them to eat a rattler?" Durken asked.

"Never killed us, did it?" said McAfee.

"Won't kill the birds either, if they stay away from the poison sacs in the head."

As they crossed the strip of brittle, blackened grass, they saw the crows and buzzards pecking greedily at the charred snakes.

"I've never seen anything like that," said Black.

"Or likely smelled it," said McAfee. The snakes were starting to rot, the dead odor mixing with the burnt buffalo grass.

"Biggs is out there somewhere in that mess." Parker pointed across the charred ground. "We'll have to do something about him and the other two. They deserve at least to be buried."

"First things first," said Tate. "You can send people after them later. Right now, we have to get into that mine."

Parker gave him an angry look but shut his mouth.

The sky darkened as they approached the mesa.

"Parker, if we get a downpour, what'll that do to the mine?" Tate said looking toward the oncoming storm. "How's the drainage?"

"You saw the entrance yesterday, dusty as an attic. When we dug the shaft, we did it right. If it rains two feet, you still won't have to swim. Any ideas about how to proceed, Willoughby?"

"I was going to suggest throwing a lit lantern down the hole so it would break and spread fire around the bottom, but after yesterday, I don't think that'll bother the snakes at all. I'll go first since I know what to look and listen for."

"I know the mine. Shouldn't I go first?"

"You know the mine, Parker, but I know the snakes. I'll go first. Any objections?"

Heads shook all around. "Well, that's it then. I'll lead the way."

They tethered the horses at the entrance to the mine and walked around the side to the path leading to the top of the mesa. The makeshift graves of Durst and Martin were undisturbed.

Tate craned his neck, studying the ground.

"No sense looking for footprints," Durken told him. "The rain yesterday took care of that for us."

Bob came huffing up the head of the trail dragging a heavy canvas bag beside him.

"Put that over here." Willoughby pointed beside the open air shaft. He snuffed the stub in his pipe and put the pipe in the breast pocket of his coat. "Parker, anything I need to know or watch for on the way down or once I hit bottom?"

"The air shaft opens into the main tunnel. It's a ten foot drop to the floor. That's about it."

Willoughby rummaged in the bag and pulled out a handful of wooden-handled cylinders thick as a thumb, each wrapped in waxed paper.

"Those Coston flares?" said Durken.

Willoughby nodded. "The genuine article.

"I ain't seen them since the war."

Willoughby slit the covering with his pocket knife and peeled the waxed paper from the flare. "I'll light this and drop it down the hole."

"I thought you said fire wouldn't help," said Black.

Willoughby looked at him over his glasses. "Fire won't help, but the light will. Before I light this and drop it in, is there any risk of explosion, Parker?"

"No gas in the Black Horse. This ain't a coal mine. The only explosion danger we ever had was from blasting powder."

"That's too bad," said Durken."A good ball of fire might end the problem."

"Who else is coming with me?"

"I'm going," said Tate.

"Me too," said McAfee, slinging the .10 gauge cross his back.

Willoughby handed a flare to each of his companions and tucked the last two in his belt. "Use the lanterns, and only light these if you have to. Fire may not scare the rattlers away, but it'll kill them nonetheless. Let's go, fellows."

He lit the flare and they watched it fall through the darkness until it bounced at the bottom and rolled to the side. Its white glow showed below as a rough circle of light. Nothing moved. Willoughby felt with his foot for the first cut in the shaft wall. He took a last look at the world and disappeared down the hole.

Parker went next. Tate hesitated and McAfee said, "Get in there, Tate. I'll bring up the rear."

"Or bring it down, more the like," said Durken.

Tate nodded and climbed into the shaft. McAfee gave him a ten-foot lead and followed.

The hand holds were cut deep enough into the rock to serve as footholds as well, but their edges were rough, and at times sharp. It was slow going. Climbing down was a touchy maneuver involving taking the hand and foot from the same side of the body and moving both down eighteen inches or so to the next pair of cuts, then switching sides and repeating the process. In no time, McAfee's back ached and his calves were burning.

He would have muttered that he was getting too old for this, but he wouldn't give Tate the satisfaction of hearing him admit it. He was near the bottom of the air shaft when Parker called out. "Your foot'll tread air next time. Let it dangle and drop the other one, then work your way down with your hands. You'll only have to drop four feet or so."

McAfee did as he was told and managed to land on his feet and stay there. He looked the wrong way, and the harsh white light of the flare blinded him for a few seconds. "Damn. I forgot how bright those things are." The Coston flare cast grotesque black shadows behind the men on the rough stone of the walls, as if they were dragging monsters after them.

"Look down," said Willoughby. McAfee looked to the tunnel floor, and saw in the dust the wavering trails of dozens of snakes and with them, the prints of bare human feet."

"We might have wiped out the snakes, but I didn't see any people with them yesterday." Tate crouched on the other side of the rails. "Over here's prints from two different pairs of boots. Durst and Martin?"

"Likely so," said McAfee. "I'd hate to think they've got more of our own working against us."

"The bare feet suggest Indians," Tate said. "I think we found the Tonapa."

"They begin and end under the air shaft. That explains how the humans got in and out, but not the snakes."

"Let's follow the tracks and see where they lead. Maybe we'll find out." Parker lit his lantern and started down the tunnel. In comparison to the flare, the lantern light was dim, but the men's eyes soon adjusted to it.

The air was dry and cool, but McAfee felt a drop of sweat run between his shoulder blades. "I don't suppose I have to tell you, but shooting your pistols in here can be as dangerous to us as anything we find. A ricochet'll kill you as easy as a direct hit. If something jumps out, let me use the scatter gun."

"There's a short spur to the right another hundred feet or so," Parker said. "We should check it."

"Yes," Tate replied. "I don't want something coming out of there and getting behind us."

"Don't worry, Tate. I got your back." Tate looked behind him to see McAfee at the end of the file, the shotgun now in his hands.

"I thought it'd be colder down here," said Willoughby.

"Ventilation pulling outside air through the tunnels warms it up a little."

"Too bad. Cold makes snakes sluggish, but this isn't cold enough."

"Here's the spur. Shine your lights in there."

Willoughby and Tate shined their lanterns. McAfee aimed the shotgun into the tunnel.

"How far back does this go?" Tate asked.

"Not far. The copper played out pretty quick in this vein." Parker stepped forward then stopped. "What the hell?"

Beyond the timbers, a round chamber had been excavated. Against the wall was a crude altar hewn from the rock. Above it was carved the crooked arrow.

No one spoke. Then Willoughby walked around the altar and crouched beside it. "No bones or snake skins, but this is a curiosity." He straightened, and as he rose he held up a ghostly translucent mass of membrane as long as he was tall in the unmistakable shape of a full-breasted woman.

The climb out of the air shaft was more difficult than the descent, but no one seemed to mind, since it took them away from the accursed place. One by one, they stood on a barrel to reach the first set of handholds and pulled themselves up and out of the tunnel. The Coston flare had burned out by this time and McAfee lit his to light the tunnel until his turn came at last to make the climb. He stood on the barrel and took a last look around him before he slung the .10 gauge across his back and reached for the cuts in the rock.

On the surface, everyone was hunkered down in a circle. "You know, Parker, we're gonna have to seal those shafts, the Black Horse Mining Company notwithstanding."

"Why not just dynamite them, Tate? Be done with it. I have the company's authority to deal with contingencies."

"Then let's get it done as soon as possible. Give those bastards one less hole to hide in."

"I still can't figure," said McAfee, "how the snakes got out of there. All the tunnels dead ended, and the main shaft was blocked by the cave-in. The only way out was the air shaft."

"I been thinking about about that," said Willoughby. "Maybe the acolytes carried them out in sacks. Or maybe the snakes just wrapped around them for the ride."

"What now?" said Black.

"Now, we go back for supplies and ride for Manville." McAfee replied.

"What about Casselman?" said Tate.

"We're more likely to find the Tonapa in Mannville. Casselman can wait a day."

"I disagree. We should…" Tate's remark was cut off by Durken pulling his Colt and fanning three shots past Tate into the rocks. A rattlesnake writhed in its death throes, but not before the wizened high priest saw through its eyes the men who had to die.

XLI

The sky above the prairie began as a pale grey at the edges and darkened to a deep coppery green overhead. Flashes of lightning darted behind the thick clouds. The wind picked up as Saylor Bungard and his flock came within sight of the handful of buildings that comprised the town of Mannville.

"Pastor," said Caleb. "We've seen this weather before. It looks like a tornado is coming. We should take shelter."

Bungard turned to Caleb and skewered him with his eyes. "It is a tool of the Adversary, brother, meant to frighten us from our course. It means we are on the righteous path."

Caleb withered under Bungard's blazing stare and hung his head. "Yes, Pastor. I misspoke."

Bungard wheeled his horse to face his congregation. "And the rest of you? Who among you lacks faith?" One by one, the followers lowered their heads. "Then let us go forth, and though the serpent bite us in the heel," he held his Bible aloft. "We shall crush his head."

He spurred his horse and trotted forth toward the town as the first fat drops of rain began to fall. In ones and twos, the flock fell in behind him. Bungard didn't look back, confident that none would desert him.

Mannville was still and the windows of the town's buildings were dark as they entered its one street. The horses began to twitch."The evil is here," Bungard said. "Be on your guard."

In front of the saloon, they saw the first of the bodies: two men. One sprawled across the boardwalk in front of the entrance, the other lay bent at the waist, over the side of a watering trough, his head and shoulders in the water. The man on the boardwalk clutched a pistol in his right hand. Shards of a broken whiskey bottle littered the rough boards around him. Another revolver lay beside the man in the trough. Their skins were the color of a deep bruise in the washed out light.

Beside the trough, a horse was tied to the hitching rail, exhausted from trying to tear its reins free. A froth of white foam dripped from its mouth and mixed with blood where the bridle had torn off an ear in the struggle. Its eyes rolled wildly in its head, searching desperately for relief.

Bungard nodded to one of his men who dismounted and picked up the pistol beside the trough. He approached the horse carefully, but it was too tired to rear. The sound of the shot was all but muffled by the pounding rain that now fell like buckshot on the muddy street. The horse fell, its head still tied to the rail, making it look as if it were gazing into the dark clouds that swirled overhead. His executioner gently laid the pistol back in the mud where he found it.

Past the street's end on a low hillock, they saw a small whitewashed chapel, the cross on its belfry shining in the occasional blaze of lightning. "There." Bungard kneed his horse and set off toward the church.

The chapel had a small hand carved placard over the entrance: *Behold, I have set before thee an open door, and no man can shut it. - Revelation 3:8.* Bungard turned the handle and found it was locked from the inside. He pounded his fist on the door. No response came from within. He knocked again more forcefully. "Have no fear. We are of the Lord." No reply came.

Bungard took a step back and brought his boot to bear on the door. It splintered with a loud crack and swung inward, crashing against the wall. He stepped inside but could see nothing at first in the dim light. He struck a match, and its sulfurous glare revealed a raft of horrors. He strode between the pews, stepping over the bodies of the dead, men, women, and children toward the altar, where a snake draped obscenely over the arms of the cross, its tongue lazily flicking in and out, tasting the air.

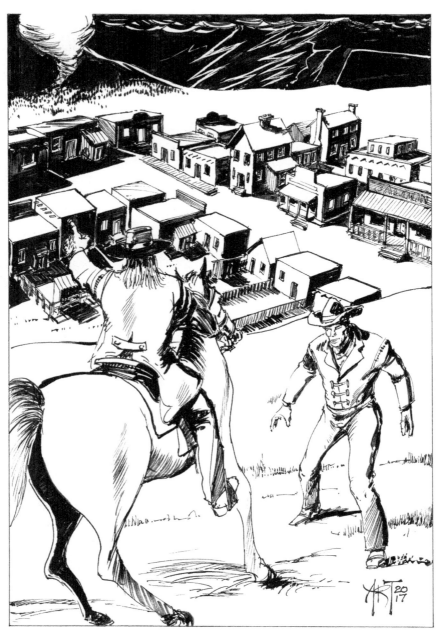

"It looks like a tornado is coming."

Its diamond eyes locked with Bungard's, and the snake slithered onto the altar, where it drew itself into a coil, its tail whirring. The Pastor lit a candle to one side of the altar and drew himself to his full height. He held his Bible before him, pointed a finger at the coiled snake, and his eyes rolled back in his head. "Nnng, nnng, zieagh, bezatt," he intoned. The rattlesnake first slowed its bobbing and swaying, then ceased altogether. Bungard continued his incantation. Slowly, the snake's head sank to the altar, and it lay still.

The minister seized the snake in his fist and dashed it to the floor. He raised his boot and brought its heel down on the serpent's head with a wet crunch. He turned to face his followers, who had crowded into the chapel. What he saw on their faces were looks of absolute horror. The light of the candle revealed what the flare of the match did not.

Bodies were sprawled over pews and in the center aisle, blackened faces, lolling tongues, and eyes staring at some far away land. "Look upon it!" Bungard shouted. "It is the Devil's work, and we are the lord's instrument to stop it once and for all!" Among the dead lay the bodies of snakes, some blown apart by gun fire, some bludgeoned, and some slashed with knives clutched in cold fingers.

One of the followers crouched beside the body of a young man and slid his revolver from its holster. He looked up to see Bungard staring at him. "What will you do with that, brother Joshua?"

Joshua's Adam's apple bobbed as he swallowed bile and fear. "We must arm ourselves, Pastor."

"What good did worldly weapons do for these people? Our weapons are not those of the flesh but of the spirit, brother. Give it to me." He held out his hand. Joshua clung to the pistol with both of his. Bungard's voice rose in pitch and volume. "Give it to me."

Joshua reluctantly handed the pistol to Bungard, who threw it across the room to clatter into a corner. "We do not need guns, nor knives, nor truncheons, nor fists when we have the word of God." He held the Bible aloft and closed his eyes in prayer. "Heavenly Father, hear our supplication as we go forth to do your will and avenge the slaughter of these your sheep. Fortify us to smite the enemy where we may find him, and to hold fast and not falter in our resolve. Amen."

Amens sounded around the chapel, but with less conviction than before. Outside, lightning struck nearby, and thunder shook the frail building. "There!" Bungard shouted. "The voice of the Lord. He is with us."

Without waiting for a response from his followers, Bungard strode through the vestibule and out the door into the pounding rain. One by one, his companions gazed around them at the ghastly tableau and filed out of the chapel. Joshua hung behind, and when all but he were gone, he retrieved the discarded pistol and shoved it into his waist band under his coat.

Apart from the road that led into Mannville, only one road led out of town, the road to the abandoned mine. Bungard rode in the lead, his flock following in twos and threes through the slashing rain. Small rivers ran through the ruts and turned the road to dense mud that sucked at the horses' hooves with every step. Rain poured from the brim of Bungard's hat, and all were soaked to their skins by the time they topped a small rise and in the flare of lightning saw the entrance to the mine.

The wind rose in its fury, sending Bungard's hat sailing from his head whipping his hair in frenzied waves. The horses began to wheel and rear, refusing to go further. Bungard dismounted. "We are not animals. We do not fear. Follow me." He turned to see them still mounted, struggling to control their horses.

"Pastor, look," said one of the flock, pointing to the east. A distant funnel cloud writhed and twisted in a black dance of death "Oh, ye of little faith," he snarled, "The Lord is with us. Who can oppose us?" and set off on foot toward the portal. His people climbed from their saddles and followed him.

Lightning flashed and showed only the dark hole in the earth, then flashed again and revealed the goddess.

Ki-No-Na-Te stood outside the opening, her golden eyes gleaming. The diamond pattern of her scales ran from her shoulder blades to the end of her tail, where a rattle vibrated like a giant krotala. On her head, living snakes twisted and danced in the wind and rain like the black cyclone on the horizon. A snake draped around her neck, suckling at her scaled breast.

Bungard locked his eyes with the diamond slits of the goddess and told his apostles, "Behold! Satan's child! Lilith the damned!"

The goddess's face split across, baring a set of wicked fangs. Her long, forked tongue slid from her mouth and bobbed and danced. She gestured with one of her clawed hands, and a river of snakes poured from the tunnel behind her, gathering around her coils.

The flock quailed in terror falling back, and Bungard said in his pulpit voice, "Stand still and see the salvation of the Lord!" Ki-No- Na-Te hissed a command, and the serpents surged across the open ground, their rattling rising beyond the sound of the storm. Bungard raised his Bible and began to chant. "Nng . . .nng . . . phnglui . . . " The twelve behind him picked up the incantation, softly at first, then swelling like the sound of the thunder. "Nng . . .nng . . . phnglui . . . Iä! Iä!"

The mass of rattlesnakes slowed and finally stopped, going limp on the wet ground. The faithful continued to chant as Bungard strode through the mass of them kicking them aside and treading on them as he went.

He pointed to the goddess and shouted. "Submit! Submit to the Living God, you spawn of the Great Serpent!"

The goddess drew back one of her leathery arms and threw something at Bungard that bounced and rolled through the mass of snakes, landing at his feet. It was the blood fresh skull of a small child.

Ki-No-Na-Te smiled wickedly and spoke in a sibilant voice words unheard in the howling wind. Bungard stopped and stared as the shaman stepped from behind her. He raised his hands and the mass of snakes began to circle around the minister, slowly at first then picking up speed like a whirlpool. Bungard resumed his chant, frantic now, but the vortex of hissing, rattling serpents continued its deadly dance.

Bungard's flock fell silent, frozen in horror as they watched the spinning circle contract. The wizened priest brought his hands together, and the circle closed, the mass of snakes climbing the screaming pastor's shins, his thighs, and his torso until he was engulfed head to toe in a rain-slick mass that wriggled like maggots at a corpse.

Bungard gave a last strangled shriek that sounded like "forsaken me" and toppled under the mound of serpents. Then the snakes turned to his followers, huddled on the hillock. Joshua pulled the revolver from his coat and cocked the hammer, knowing they could never run fast enough or far enough. He fired five times, each shot to the head of another of his companions, granting each a merciful death. "I'm sorry," he told the other six, and put the barrel of the gun in his mouth.

The hammer fell on an empty chamber.

XLII

Durken and McAfee spent the evening and the rest of the night holed up in the Copper Queen sharing a bottle. "Damned shame we couldn't ride for Mannville right away."

Durken rolled his shot glass between his thumb and fore finger. "Indians, I don't mind so much; snakes, I don't mind so much, but I don't want to chance a twister. Especially since I never heard of one in Utah before."

"They have them here, but they're rare. The one we saw was gyrating, moving across the horizon. It's when they're straight up and down that they're headed for you."

"But when the weather brews up one, there's always the chance of more. Besides," he said, filling his glass, "where would you rather spend the night? Out in the saddle in the dark with the wind and the rain, or in this dry, well-lit place with this bottle?"

"I'd agree if it weren't for the company." McAfee looked across the saloon to the table where Willoughby was taking Parker and his deputies at five-card stud. Black and Tate sat in huddled conversation at a table in the corner. "What do you suppose those two are cooking up?"

"Nothing good, I expect," Durken stared into the mirror. "But we're about to find out."

Tate and Black pushed their chairs away from the table and crossed the room. Tate leaned against the bar beside Durken. "We have to send a message to our chief. He hasn't heard from us for days."

"I suppose that could be arranged. Want to do that right now?"

"If the line's clear."

"All right." Durken gulped down the last of his whiskey and set his glass on the bar. "You two wait here. McAfee, bring Tate and Black to the telegraph station in five minutes." He turned to Tate. "I'll get the telegraph working, and you can send your message. McAfee and I'll both be there when you send it."

"You can't be privy to a Secret Service message," Black sputtered. "It's classified."

Durken turned back to the bar and poured himself another shot. "And I thought we were on the same side. If it's that secret, maybe you shouldn't send it over the wires at all."

Tate and Black stepped back a few feet and spoke in hushed tones. "All right, Durken. We have to send that message. You and your partner can eavesdrop if you want."

McAfee took his watch from his vest pocket. "Five minutes."

Durken nodded, pulled a slicker over his head, and strode out into the pelting rain.

"I'm surprised you two have lived as long as you have," said Black.

"Funny," said McAfee, "I was just thinking the same about you."

XLIII

Evans saw the gaudy railroad car in a flash of lightning and although he'd been told about it in advance, he was still surprised at the carnival look of it, and even more surprised at the pair of sentries that stood guard beside the iron steps to its platform.

He had ridden hard, stopping nowhere but Casselman, and there only because he saw a Cavalry unit encamped outside the town and traded his weary horse for a fresh one and got some cheese and bread to eat in the saddle.

As Evans approached the rail car, the sentries stepped together barring the stairs and brought their carbines to port arms. "State your business." said the one on the left.

"Private Evans with a message for General Sherman from Lieutenant McAfee."

The sentry who had spoken turned and stepped up the clanging stairs onto the platform. He knocked at the door and stuck his head in when it opened. He nodded and turned to Evans. "Come up, Private."

Evans stepped through the door into a coach dimly lit by a fire burning to one side in a small fireplace. Sherman slumped in a chair, warming the soles of his boots on the grate. Evans, recognizing the General, snapped to attention and saluted.

"At ease. Come over, son," said Sherman never looking away from the dancing flames. "Pull up a chair. I expect you're soaked through."

Evans dragged a dainty chair with gilded legs to the hearth and sat heavily in it, dripping onto the carpet. "Thank you, sir. It's been quite a time." He drew the oilskin bundle from inside his blouse and offered it to Sherman, who looked at it but didn't take it immediately.

"You know, Private…Evans is it? Whoever said 'ignorance is bliss' spoke the most profound wisdom. As soon as I take that from you, I'm obligated to open it and read it. And I know it's going to cause me an ache in my head, and a pain in my ass, isn't it?"

"I expect so, General."

"Why don't you open it up and read it to me, Evans. I left my spectacles in the other room."

Evans read, and at one point Sherman closed his eyes. Evans read a little longer then paused and tilted his head to look at the General's face. One eye opened and Sherman said, "Don't stop now, son, you've finally got my interest."

When Evans finished reading the account, Sherman stared into the fire, which had burned to embers. He rose and crossed to the ornate table that served as his desk. "When was the last time you slept, Private?"

"Truth be told, two days, sir. I couldn't sleep after what I saw."

"I understand. Maybe this will help." Sherman crossed to the table and poured a stiff drink for each of them. He handed one to Evans and said, "You can sleep in my bed in the next room. I'll need you fresh to take a message back in the morning."

"Sir, where will you sleep?"

Sherman rubbed the back of his hand over a day's dark stubble. "I don't expect I will. I'll be up all night deciding what message to send back. And I thought war was hell."

XLIV

In the telegraph office, Durken replaced the wet cell battery he'd hidden in a shed behind the building. As soon as he hooked up the wires, the key began to chatter. Some of the talk was about damage from the tornado and requests for help. The code came for Collinsville to receive a message. Durken tapped the code to receive, and grabbed the stub of a pencil from the counter.

The message was for Tate: REPORT STATUS IMMEDIATELY STOP THIRD NOTICE STOP HAVE YOU LOCATED OBJECT STOP FLINTLOCK.

It took all of Durken's self-control to not tap out his own message to McMonagle and tell him where to shove his head. He tapped the code for receipt of the message and rolled a cigarette while he waited for McAfee, Tate, and Black and listened to the rattle of the telegraph key.

The three came into the telegraph station a few minutes later, shaking off water from the storm outside. Durken handed the slip of paper with the message to Tate. You better answer him quick, Tate. This fellow seems a tad impatient."

"You have no idea." Tate took off his hat and set it on the desk beside the telegraph key. He played a staccato tattoo on the unit, a series of numbers and letters.

"What's that?" McAfee said.

"A priority code to clear the line for a government transmission."

McAfee's eyes darted to Durken who nodded, letting him know it was committed to memory for future convenience. Tate waited a moment, then the notification of an open line came through.

After naming the U. S. Secret Service, New York City, as recipient, Tate sent a terse message: FLINTLOCK EYES STOP COLLINSVILLE TORNADO DELAYED SEARCH STOP CONTACT WITHIN DAYS STOP NOTIFY MARIONETTE STOP ARROWHEAD.

Tate ended the message, signing off the line. "Now, we wait for a reply. The men sat in silence for five minutes, ten, then the key rattled. RECEIVED ACKNOWLEDGED STOP FLINTLOCK. "That's it," said Tate, standing. "Let's go, Black." The pair left the telegraph office and McAfee watched them through the window until they crossed the street and went into the Copper Queen.

"You know something ain't right about this."

"I don't doubt that the Secret Service has an operator by the telegraph day and night, but relaying the message from station to station should've taken a lot longer than five minutes each way. That message was picked up and answered by somebody close by."

Durken nodded. "Maybe we should wait a while to disconnect the battery. Who knows what else might come over the line."

"Sounds sensible."

"I'll stay here. You go keep an eye on Tate and Black."

McAfee pulled his slicker over his hat and stepped out into the storm. Durken rolled another cigarette and tipped his chair back against the wall. He stared at the silent telegraph key, then remembering something Maggie always said about watched pots, he studied the glowing end of his cigarette and waited.

McAfee returned to the Copper Queen in time to hear Parker say to Tate, "The storm's letting up. We should be able to make Manville in four hours or so unless the road's washed out somewhere in between."

"That'd be good." He turned to McAfee. "Wouldn't you say, so, Lieutenant?" Tate seemed to put more emphasis on the last word than was necessary, but McAfee let it go by. "I know Mannville's out of your bailiwick, Parker. You ever been there?"

"No, but it shouldn't be too hard to find. Not much else out that way, mostly open country. We can leave at sunup."

The poker game had broken up and Willoughby was sitting alone at the table playing Solitaire. His suit piles were nearly up to the face cards when McAfee pulled up a chair. McAfee looked across the room and saw Tate and Black, heads together again, talking quietly.

"So tell me, Willoughby, since you know who Flintlock is, who's Marionette?"

Willoughby's brow creased in thought. "Marionette. Can't say I ever heard that monicker." He played the King of Hearts, finishing the suit. Another play freed the Jack, Queen, and King of Spades. "Well that game's done." He leaned back in his chair.

"You aren't going to finish? Beat the Devil?"

Willoughby took off his spectacles and rubbed the bridge of his nose with a thumb and forefinger. "From all I've ever seen, McAfee, we never beat the Devil. Best we can do is a draw; hold him back for a day. He never quits trying."

"Kinda like you throwing in with Tate."

Willoughby nodded. "That or hang from the same tree with Magnus. Live another day."

He laid the last of the cards on the table. "We may find this source that Tate's talking about, and if we do, what then?"

"I suppose we'll figure that out when the time comes."

XLV

The morning dawned grey and cold. McAfee and Durken came downstairs to find Parker and his deputies drinking coffee at a table in the saloon. The cowboys poured coffee for themselves and sat. Durken poured a dollop of whiskey from the bottle in the middle of the table, and McAfee did the same.

"How's the leg?" Parker asked.

"Hurts more like a toothache and less like a gunshot."

"Durken and I've been talking it over. Is there any dynamite here, left over from the mining operation?"

"Nope, none that I know of. The company took everything useful when they closed the mine."

"If we find the lair, we'll have to call for supplies."

"How much longer do Tate and Black think they can keep this business quiet? What's the old saying? 'Three can keep a secret…'"

McAfee finished the quotation. "'If two of them are dead.' The only reason it's been under wraps this long is it's happened out here and not in some big town full of people."

"That and the fact that the snakes don't leave any witnesses. Maybe we ought to consider ourselves lucky and just sit this one out."

"And let Tate and Black have a free hand?" Durken spat on the floor. "I want those two where I can see them."

Parker nodded then raised his chin toward the stairs. "And here they come now."

Tate and Black came downstairs already wearing their dusters over their suits.

"Want some coffee, boys?" Parker pointed to the pot. "Should still be warm."

"No time," said Tate. "Let's get going."

The ride took every minute of Parker's predicted four hours, traveling across empty expanses of prairie and brush with the distant mountains to one hand and an infinite flat horizon to the other. At one point, they crossed a quarter-mile strip of ground where a funnel cloud passed through the night before, leaving almost nothing but bare earth. "Looks like the March," said McAfee.

"No," said Durken. "There's too much grass left."

The road into Mannville was awash with mud, showing no tracks into or out of the town. "Looks as if nobody's been by this way since last night," Tate said.

"Maybe they've got better sense than we do," said McAfee. "The weather doesn't look too promising. I'd guess they're still holed up from the twister."

"Well, you can ask them yourself in a few minutes." Parker pointed down the road. "That's Mannville up ahead." The roofs of the town showed over the horizon like the hats of people hiding behind a rock. The image blurred, and Parker said. "Oh, hell. Here comes the rain again." The hazy curtain drifted toward the riders as the horses plodded through the mud until they met the line of raindrops.

"Does it always rain this much around here?" Black pulled up the collar of his duster around his chin.

"Not usually. This weather's strange, especially for this time of year."

As they rode into the town, Black called out, "Hello! Territory Sheriff! Anyone here?" There was no answer. He shouted again, a little louder, but still got no response.

"Doesn't look good," McAfee drew his coat back, uncovering his holster.

"Nope," Durken replied, sliding the shotgun from its scabbard.

Manville's main street curved to the left around a slight rise, and as they rounded the bend, they saw the dead horse. Looking closer, through the rain, they saw the two dead men. Willoughby slid from his saddle and picked his way through the mud to the corpses.

He tore open the shirt of the man lying on the boardwalk. "Like the others we've seen. Bites all over him." He gestured to the body in the trough. "From the color of his hands, I'd say this one didn't drown, either." Willoughby grabbed the dead man's collar and pulled him from the trough. The corpse fell on its back, face black and eyes bulging. Fang marks showed on his cheek and his throat.

"Snakes didn't kill the horse," Durken said. "Looks like a bullet hole in his head.

Willoughby crouched over the dead animal; he opened his Case knife and cut the animal's reins. Its head splashed in the mud, spattering his boots. "Well, McAfee, do we search for survivors?"

"We'd better." Tate dropped from his horse. "Anybody alive here can tell us what happened."

"I think we already know, Tate," said Parker. "But if anyone's still alive here, I have a duty to see they stay that way." He dismounted. "Let's split up and search all the buildings."

A half hour's canvassing of the cluster of stores and businesses turned up no one, dead or alive. The men gathered in the street. "That leaves the church." Parker pointed up the hill to the small whitewashed chapel. Without a word, the party mounted up and headed up the hill.

The chapel was as Bungard and his flock had found it.

"What do you think, Sheriff?" McAfee stood just inside the vestibule, Durken beside him.

"Maybe they all came into the church because of the tornado, and then the attack came."

"That makes sense. Fast as these devils move, folks wouldn't have had time to gather here, even if they saw them coming."

"We have to get to that mine, Parker," said Tate, stepping over corpses in the aisle.

McAfee nodded. "I agree. Let's ride."

Tate studied the mud as they rode along. "Looks like no tracks on this road either."

"Storm would have washed them away. You expecting to find some?" McAfee said, eyeing him suspiciously.

Tate shook his head. "No, just thinking out loud."

"Is that like your mouth moving while you read?"

Tate gave McAfee his cold smile. "We can't all be as clever as you,

Lieutenant." He nudged his horse in the side and pulled ahead of McAfee and Durken. Black followed after him.

"That's the second time he's called me that in a day. I wonder why?"

"Always something going on with that one," said Durken. "You never quite see all the way around him."

McAfee nodded. "We better watch him close. Him and Black. Do you trust Willoughby?" The snake handler was riding in the lead conversing with Parker.

"Up to a point; he's thrown in with us, it seems, but you notice Tate hasn't fired him yet."

"I know. That's what worries me."

"Yep." Durken raised his head. "Look." He pointed ahead to dark specks wheeling in the grey sky. "Hell of a lot of birds."

"That can mean only one thing...hell of a lot of food. Parker! Up ahead."

"I see them," the sheriff replied. "As if there weren't enough dead already."

In minutes, they came upon a hideous scene. Corpses were sprawled on the grassy sward, faces frozen in agony and terror, some blackened and some white as a fish belly. The hungry crows pecked at the pale flesh but left the discolored bodies alone. Parker fired two shots and the birds took wing, only to light again nearby, to watch and wait for another chance at the deadly banquet.

"I count twelve," said Black.

"There's another one over here," Bob called out. It was Bungard, but he couldn't be recognized by his face, which had more fang marks than the men could count. They knew it was the minister because he still clutched his rain-soaked Bible in his left hand.

"It's the preacher," said Durken, climbing from his saddle.

"Looks like he's been beat with a morning star," McAfee noted.

"A what?" asked Parker.

"A medieval weapon," Tate replied before McAfee could speak. "A spiked ball on a chain. Very effective."

"What was the preacher doing here with his followers, Tate?" Durken said with a tone in his voice McAfee recognized as cold menace. "How did he know to come here?"

"I don't have the slightest notion. I..."

Tate's sentence was interrupted by Durken grabbing him by the coat, pulling him from the saddle, and throwing him to the ground. Black fumbled under his duster for his pistol, and McAfee pulled the shotgun from Durken's saddle. The click of the hammers froze Black in mid-draw.

"Go on, Black. Pull on us." He grinned. "Please."

Parker and his men were as stunned as Black. None of them moved. Durken dragged Tate through the mud by his collar until his eyes were inches from the bloated pulpy mass of Bungard's face. "This is your doing, Tate. You sent those people here. They're all dead, and for what?" He pulled his Colt and stuck the barrel in the agent's ear. "Tell me why I shouldn't kill you here and now." He cocked the hammer.

Tate smiled his cold smile, but Durken didn't see it, or he would have pulled the trigger. "If you listen hard, you'll hear the reason why, Lieutenant."

Durken glanced at McAfee, who was looking behind him. "Horses."

A group of riders approached, fifteen in all, indistinct in the rain. As they came closer, McAfee recognized Cavalry uniforms. In the lead was a soldier in an officer's hat with a bushy fox tail trailing from its band. They drew abreast of the party, and the officer raised his hand to halt. The soldiers all carried Winchesters across their saddles.

"Which of you is Durken, and which if you McAfee?" the officer said.

"I'm McAfee." He pointed, keeping the forefinger of his other hand around the triggers of the shotgun. "He's Durken."

"I'm Colbert." He looked pointedly at Durken. "Please holster your sidearm, Lieutenant." Durken didn't move.

"That's Captain Colbert," Tate said. Colbert pulled aside the collar of his slicker and showed a pair of gold bars. Tate snickered. "And that was an order... Lieutenant."

Durken eased the hammer of his pistol down, then with a snap of his wrist slammed the barrel across the bridge of Tate's nose. Tate rolled in the mud groaning, clutching his face. Blood oozed between his fingers. Durken stood, holstered his revolver, and gave a slouching salute. "Yes, sir, Captain. Any other orders?"

XLVI

"So Marionette was an it, not a who." Durken bit a chew of tobacco from the plug and stuffed it back into his pocket, careful to keep it from getting wet in the drizzling rain that had fallen off and on since the Cavalry arrived.

"I should've figured it out. Puppets. Pulling strings."

"That's why Tate was so smug."

"He doesn't look so smug now." McAfee pointed with his chin to Tate, who was talking earnestly with Colbert. His nose had swollen to nearly twice its size and seemed in danger of bursting. Tate was clearly agitated, flapping his arms as he spoke to Colbert who stood, impassive, with his arms folded across his chest. Five of the soldiers stood in a rough arc, ten feet apart, staring at McAfee and Durken and holding rifles at port arms.

"Them blue bellies're spread out enough to make it a chore to shoot them all, even as good as we are."

McAfee nodded. "I wouldn't make any sudden moves."

"Agreed."

"We're lieutenants. If we said, 'at ease,' do you think they'd follow the order?"

"Do you?"

"Cold day in hell."

"There you go."

Colbert had come with papers signed by the Secretary of War giving him command of the operation and relieving Durken and McAfee of their duties. They were to report to General Sherman and then be decommissioned once again to civilian status.

"I bet the General had a few choice words to say about all this." McAfee reached into his coat for his tobacco, halted, and looked over to the soldiers. He held one hand palm up while he slowly drew out the leather pouch with the other. He grinned. "Easy, fellas."

Tate gave a final flail of his arms and stalked off in disgust. Colbert strode over to Durken and McAfee. "Tate wants you two imprisoned, or shot if that can be arranged, but my orders are simply to relieve you and send you back to General Sherman unmolested. If you go willingly, no problem. If you resist, Agent Tate may get his wish, one way or the other."

Durken turned to McAfee. "You know, I'm starting to miss Charlie's cooking."

McAfee nodded. "Me too, and it's been a while since I've seen Sarah."

"It's settled then?"

"Yep," said Durken. "We know how to follow orders."

"And you know that you are to say nothing about this affair to anyone."

"We figured as much," said, McAfee, "And Captain, I hope you know what you're getting into with Tate. He doesn't always tell the whole story up front."

"Doesn't keeping this business quiet put people in danger?" Durken looked over his shoulder to where Tate and Black stood, glaring at him. "Those two don't seem to much care about it."

"I'm hopeful that we'll end this." He glanced at the two pack horses laden with equipment. "Today."

"We wish you well, Captain Colbert," said McAfee. "Can we leave now?"

"The sooner the better, and take Parker and his deputies with you."

McAfee saluted, and Durken touched the brim of his hat. "Come on, Parker," he called to the sheriff, "let's go home."

As Mannville came into sight, Parker said, "What are they going to do about those dead people in the town?"

"I imagine Black'll take lots of pictures. Maybe they'll take the bodies with them to examine," McAfee said.

"I'm starting to think Jud had the right idea." Parker shook his head. "Those people have suffered enough without the indignity of being stripped and photographed and who knows what else."

"There's a remedy for that," said Durken.

Parker nodded. "Yes, there is."

Later, as they stood outside the Mannville chapel, Parker, Durken, and McAfee watched as the deputies dragged the two corpses from the street inside. Parker made a torch from a broken pick handle and cloth soaked in kerosene. He lit it with a match and threw it through the splintered door into the vestibule.

The men waited in silence until the whole church was engulfed in crackling orange flames before mounting their horses and riding out of town.

"Tate and Black'll be upset," said Bob, looking over his shoulder at the column of smoke behind them.

"Good," Parker replied. "Time they had a turn."

Instead of returning to Collinsville, Durken, McAfee, and Parker decided to take a cross-country route in the hope of making Casselman by dark. "I envy you two," Parker said. "I wish I was shut of this business, but I still have to deal with those dead soldiers and a town that's likely in a panic by now."

"There is that," Durken said. "Duty. In some ways, I envy you, Parker. We have to ride away and leave Tate to his…" he turned to McAfee. "What's that word you like to use for deviltry?"

"Machinations," McAfee said. "And I don't like it any better than you do, but we can't just pull guns on Colbert and his men because he pulled rank on us."

"Yep. We know how to follow orders."

"God damned Army."

"No, God damned politicians who pull the marionettes' strings."

"Got that right."

XLVII

L iam was pouring drinks for a gang of cowboys celebrating payday when the man with the scar on his forehead came into the Silver Dollar. He set the bottle down and moved up the bar where the man…Ketchum? Was that his name? …stood waiting.

"You're that fellow looking for his brother-in-law, ain't you?"

Ketchum nodded. "Any word on him and his friend?"

"Matter of fact, Sheriff Bennet was in here yesterday. Said if I saw you to send you over to his office."

A hopeful look swept across Ketchum's features. "Was there news?"

Liam gave Ketchum his best blank face. "I couldn't say, my friend. You'll have to ask the sheriff."

"Much obliged," Ketchum said, and left the Silver Dollar for the jail.

Liam shook his head sadly. Far be it from me, he thought, to deliver that kind of news if I don't have to. He poured himself a shot of whiskey and raised his glass to the memory of the dead.

Ketchum found the Sheriff behind his desk in the jail. Shub, his deputy, dozed in a chair propped against the wall. "Sheriff Bennet? I'm Jake Ketchum. The bartender down the street said you have news for me."

Bennet rose to his full height. "I'm sorry to have to tell you this, Mister Ketchum, but your brother-in-law and his friend are dead."

Ketchum's face sank. "I was afraid that's how it was. How did it happen?"

"I don't have any details, except that their remains and their belongings are in the custody of Sheriff Curtis Parker in Collinsville. That's in the Utah Territory."

"I guess I'll go and collect their things. The trip'll give me time to figure out how to tell my wife her baby brother's dead."

Bennet ran his hand through his iron-grey hair. "Mister Ketchum, I've had to give plenty of people that news the last twenty years. I always found the best way is to just say it. Most people are stronger than we give them credit. You have my sympathy for your loss."

"Thank you, Sheriff," Ketchum said, head down, and walked past the still sleeping Shub out the door and into the street.

XLVIII

Bob and Roy, Parker's deputies, had the unwelcome task of bringing the bodies of Durst and Martin to Collinsville. Before they could do that, they had to climb the mesa and drag away the rocks that kept the scavengers away from the remains, wrapped in blood-soaked blankets. "They're buried," Roy grumbled. "Why not just leave them that way?"

Sheriff says we have to bring them to town. That Federal wants the bodies to study or something."

"Not much to study after two barrels of that .10 gauge."

"No argument there." Bob wiped the sweat from his forehead with the back of his hand. He would have used his neckerchief, but it was pulled up over his mouth and nose to block the stench of the dead men.

The last rocks pulled away, the remains, wrapped in saddle blankets, made a pair of short bundles in the shallow grave. They lifted them out, careful to not allow the corners of a blanket to come undone and spill their grisly content, but Roy lost hold on his end and the blanket fell open, spilling ropy coils of intestine from a burst abdomen. Roy cried out, pulled his six-gun, and fired three shots into the gory mass before Bob slapped the gun from his hand.

"What the hell's the matter with you?"

Roy laughed nervously. "I thought they was snakes."

Bob stared at the mound of entrails. "Yeah, I guess they do look like it at that." He scooped the guts up with a shovel and dumped them back onto the blanket. The remains were set on a canvas tarpaulin and bound with rope.

"That ought to hold them," said Roy, pulling the rope tight on the last knot.

"Like as if they're planning to escape," Bob japed. "Dead is dead, Roy."

"Yeah, but don't it give you the willies being up here? Knowing what was down below, I mean."

"Naah," Bob said. "Whatever was down there's gone now. Sheriff said so. Come on. Help me tote these sons-of-bitches down the hill." Bob didn't want to admit it, but the further they got from the Black Horse Mine, the better he liked it.

XLIX

"**N**ow, Agent Tate, before I risk my men's lives on this operation," Colbert looked pointedly over his shoulder to the sight of his men arranging the thirteen blanket-wrapped corpses in a neat row. "I need you to tell me just exactly what is our objective." Captain Colbert leaned forward toward the fire, his hands around a cup of steaming coffee.

"What have you been told so far?"

"That we were to come here and 'render support and assistance' in your capture of an enemy. Now, am I correct that the enemy is holed up in that mine?"

"Yes, we believe so."

"'We' being you and Black."

"And Willoughby." Tate took a long breath as if he were about to dive into a deep lake and launched into a carefully rehearsed story. "In ancient Indian lore . . ."

Colbert listened for nearly a half hour, and when Tate finished his narrative, Colbert leaned back, looked up at the sky, looked into the fire, then leveled his gaze on Tate. "Now, Tate, tell me the real reason we're out here."

Tate's expression froze. "What do you mean, Captain?"

"McAfee was right when he said you never give the whole picture. I was in Military Intelligence in the war, Tate. Your story doesn't even skim the surface. If this Snake Mother controlling an army of rattlers was the main issue, why not just shoot her, it, whatever? Why do we have to take her alive so she can still be a threat? My men don't move until I know."

Neither spoke for a couple of minutes. Finally, Tate nodded his head, having reached some momentous decision. "All right, Colbert. I'll tell you. There was at least one attack before the one in Casselman, a cavalry patrol from Silver Forks. There was a survivor."

"You mean somebody escaped?"

"Not an escapee, Colbert, a survivor. There's a big difference." Tate took a thin cheroot from his jacket and leaned toward the fire, taking a splint of wood from the fire's edge and lighting his cigar with it. "He didn't escape. He was let go with a purpose."

L

When the patrol didn't return to the Silver Forks outpost, a search party was dispatched. The men rode for an entire day before they saw a hatless man walking alone across a sunburned strip of land. As they came closer, they realized he was in a cavalry uniform. As he came closer, they could see his blouse was torn and his holster empty, bloodied knees showed through shredded trousers. As they came closer, they could see the slack jaw and vacant eyes of a man in a daze.

The soldiers dismounted and approached him carefully. Bruckner, the sergeant in charge, asked him, "What's happened, Private? Where's your unit?"

"My unit." the private said pronouncing every syllable.

"What's happened to you, son?"

The private said something too faint for the sergeant to hear him that sounded like "obey." Bruckner turned to his men. "Bring a canteen. He... Sweet Jesus!"

The sergeant's head jerked back at the flash of a blade that barely missed his throat. He grabbed the private's knife hand and twisted it behind his back as he drove his elbow into the soldier's temple. The private fell to the ground and lay still.

"Tie him up." Bruckner picked up the knife. Along the edge was a bluish stain. He'd seen enough in his time to know a poisoned blade when he saw it. "We'll take him back to the outpost and get to the bottom of this."

For three days and nights, the private, whose name was Conwell, alternated between lying catatonic on the bunk in his cell in the blockhouse and bouncing off the walls and bars foaming at the mouth and raving about serving the goddess and obeying the master. "Kill you! Kill you all," he screamed, trying to reach through the bars at his guards.

In the meantime, the search party found the missing patrol, every man among them dead from dozens of snake bites in what looked like a disassembled encampment. On the fourth day, the guards found Conwell curled up on the floor clutching his head with one hand and his stomach with the other. On the fifth day, he woke up sensible, and that's when he told as much of his story as he could recall. His commander Lieutenant Copley and Bruckner heard his story in his cell:

"We were riding north half a day out when we found what looked like a redskin camp. There was a fire pit, a couple of lean-tos and one big tipi.

When we rode in, there was no one there, but the ashes in the fire were still warm. A few of us were about to go into the wigwam when we heard a voice kinda half chanting half singing in Indian lingo. We all turned around and saw an old man in some kind of cape looked like it was made of snakeskin.

"I know a little Cherokee and some Paiute, but whatever language he was singing wasn't either of those or any other language I ever heard. He was so wrinkled his skin looked like scales itself, and his hair was pure white. Then he raised his hands, and rattlesnakes came out of the ground all around us. Everybody was shooting and screaming, and I saw the old man point at me. The snakes bit the hell out of the others, but they left me alone.

"What I should've done was shoot the old man, but by the time I thought of it, I was out of bullets. Everybody else was lying on the ground dead or dying, and the old man just stood pointing at me and singing in that weird language. And then behind me I heard the flap open in the tipi, and before I could turn to look, hands like claws grabbed me and threw me on the ground. I looked up into a face…that face, dear God…like something out of a nightmare.

"It was a woman's face, but her skin was scaly and her eyes were diamond slits like a rattler's. Her mouth was as wide as a barn door and had big fangs. Instead of hair, she had a head full of snakes all twisting and turning. Then she let out that long, forked tongue of hers and started licking my face, but she wasn't just licking it. She was painting it with her slimy spit. I felt myself going out. It was like when I got that arrow through me and the doc gave me laudanum; it made me sleep and dream, and I don't remember anything that happened after that. Next thing I knew, I woke up here this morning."

Copley spoke up. "You don't remember walking without food and water, trying to kill the members of the search party?"

Conwell shook his head. "No, Sir, I don't recall any of it."

"We took a rabbit out of the cook's pen and just scratched him with that knife you had," Sergeant Bruckner added. "He was dead in seconds. That's some powerful poison on that blade. You don't know where you got it?"

"No, Sergeant. Maybe I picked it up in the Indian camp when I… Aaaugh!" A rattlesnake hung from Conwell's neck, its fangs buried just under his chin.

Bruckner's hand shot out as fast as the striking snake and yanked the rattler away. He swung it around his head and dashed its brains out against the bars of the cell. Conwell fell sideways onto the cot, his eyes glazed over, and Bruckner knew he was dead.

"Where did that snake come from, Sergeant?" The Lieutenant stood staring at the last death throes of the serpent.

"Damned if I know, Lieutenant. Must've got into his blankets somehow."

"Have him buried immediately. Don't say a word about how he died." He opened the cell door and turned as he left. "I have to send a telegram."

LI

"Let me guess," said Colbert. "He sent the telegram to you."

Tate shook his head. "No, he sent it to my superiors in New York."

Colbert nodded. "Order one-aught-seven."

"That's the one."

"And that's why you're here and I'm here."

"But you still haven't answered my question, Tate. What's the real reason we're out here? To learn how to control the rattlers?"

"It's not just control of the snakes. That could be useful, but sending a pack of rattlesnakes onto a battlefield would be like firing a shotgun into a street fight. They'd likely kill as many of our men as theirs." Tate took a pull on his cheroot and let the image sink in.

"We have to capture this Snake Mother alive for study. Her venom, if that's what it is, is a powerful hypnotic. Better still, it seems to be addictive. Conwell's symptoms on the fourth day mirror those of people withdrawing from opium addiction. If we can catch her, Willoughby can extract the substance, and we can analyze it to use against our enemies. An addictive hypnotic...imagine the potential."

"Willoughby can't do that if she's dead?"

"He could, but a dead snake can't make any more venom. Alive, she'll be an ongoing source."

Colbert nodded. "Just like milking a cow. What about the old man and his followers?"

"If they resist capture, kill them."

Black led a half dozen of the soldiers over a rise a hundred yards away where the mine's only vent shaft stood, covered by a half dozen planks crudely nailed together. Warning signs about the open shaft were lying on the ground. Blown down by the vicious storm winds. Black smiled with satisfaction. The planks were undisturbed, which meant the vent, the only one according to the map he held in his hand, wasn't being used as an entrance or an exit.

"Pull up the planks," he directed. "We need the hole open. But keep the boards handy. We'll be closing it up again."

Two soldiers set to prying the heavy planks loose while others unloaded one of the pack mules. They brought a pair of oaken kegs to the edge of the vent. Willoughby raised a hatchet over his head and brought it down on the top of the first, then the second, splitting the barrels open. Both were filled with yellow powder.

"Sulfur," said Willoughby with a satisfied nod. "Fire and brimstone."

He took a pair of Colson flares from his pack and thrust one into each keg. Two soldiers fashioned a sling out of rope to lower the sulfur one keg over the other while another pair assembled a tripod with a pulley over the hole. Willoughby wrapped a length of dynamite fuse around each of the flares. The fuse would play out as the kegs were lowered seventy feet, according to the mine map to the tunnel below.

The soldiers swung the kegs over the opening. "Careful now," said Willoughby. "Don't let them tip and spill, and whatever you do, don't let them break before they get to the bottom." He turned to Black. "You know what to do. I have to get back to the entrance."

Black nodded. "I'll wait for your signal."

At the mine entrance, Tate supervised the laying out of a heavy fisherman's net on the ground outside the opening. A larger version of the tripod at the vent stood over it. "When she comes out, your men haul on the ropes, and we catch her in the net."

"If she comes out. You seem pretty sure she's in there, Tate."

"I'm betting my career on it. Ah, here comes Willoughby."

Willoughby hurried over, puffing at his pipe. "They should have everything in place at the vent. We'll smoke them out, and she'll come with them."

"Make sure your men wear those masks Willoughby gave them. Keep their faces covered."

Colbert strode over to the trench his men had dug and filled with kerosene. Beyond it, soldiers stood with double-barreled shotguns in case any snakes got past the fire. "Looks ready here."

Tate nodded. "Give the signal."

Two pistol shots rang out. At the vent, Black put a match to the fuse and watched the sputtering fire disappear between the planks the soldiers had quickly hammered back into place. Within two minutes, the fuse lit the flares, which set the sulfur burning in the barrels, filling the tunnel with thick, choking smoke.

"Get back from the opening," Black warned. "You don't want to breathe any of that."

On the other side of the bluff at the entrance, Tate and Colbert watched and waited. All eyes were on the dark tunnel. The flames danced in the trench. Smoke began to trickle from the opening, but no snakes could be seen, and no Snake Mother came from the tunnel.

Colbert turned to Tate. "Looks like you lost your bet, Agent Tate."

"Don't give up yet, Captain. She may show up yet. I'm sure…" Tate's words ended abruptly at a sound from behind him that froze his blood, a keening, sing-song chant in a forgotten language. The men turned to see a wizened man in a full length cape fifty yards away. He raised his hands, and the grass around him came alive.

Tate stared in horror as the wave of snakes surged across the open space between them. Colbert drew his pistol and fired at the shaman, but braves stood up and closed around him in a shielding circle, three of them falling to Colbert's bullets.

Tate saw the old man point to him, and the rattlesnakes slithered over his boots and around his feet, but left him unbitten. Behind the shaman, a shape rose from the grass and slithered toward him with a murderous grace. Behind him, Willoughby fell under a mass of scaly horrors.

All around him Tate heard screams and gunfire, but his eyes were fixed on the diamond pupils of the scaled creature that wrapped her arms around him, and the gaping mouth that opened to a forked tongue that danced around his face. The screams faded and the sound of the guns seemed to echo down an ever longer tunnel until Tate heard no more.

LII

It was all but dark when Durken, McAfee, and Parker neared Casselman. They could see lanterns glowing on the road at the edge of town. As they got closer, they could make out a wagon pulled across it, blocking the way. Three soldiers slouched against the wagon, their rifles propped beside them. They straightened up when they saw the riders.

"Halt," said one of them. "This road is closed by order of the U. S. Army."

"I'm Sheriff Curtis Parker, and these men are Lieutenants McAfee and Durken."

The soldier held up his lantern and Parker pulled back his coat to reveal his badge. "Oh, well, that's different. We were told you'd be coming through." He turned to his companions. "Come on, boys, let's clear the way." The three of them pushed the wagon aside and let the riders pass. As they rode by, McAfee asked, "How many of you are there?"

"Three squads. We have the locals bottled up in the town."

McAfee didn't reply. He just kneed Sweetheart in the ribs and trotted away.

They tied their horses to a hitching rail in front of the nameless saloon. McAfee noted that the floozies were absent from the veranda overhead. As they started into the saloon, a middle-aged couple came running up to them. "Sheriff! Sheriff! Thank God you're here. They won't let us leave."

"Who won't let you leave?"

"The soldiers. They said we have to stay here. We don't want to die like those people in the wagon or that gang of soldiers. But they said we have to stay here. Bill Cobb tried to ride around the blockade, and they shot him right off his horse. Help us, Sheriff, please."

"You're Tom Gergen, right?" The man nodded and Parker put a reassuring hand on his shoulder. "I just got here, Tom. I'm going to get the lay of the land, and then I'll see what I can do about this. In the meantime, shut yourself inside and stay there. Come on," Parker said to the cowboys and headed into the saloon, leaving Gergen and his wife staring after them.

Inside the saloon, twenty or more men were leaning against the bar or sitting in knots at the tables. They all looked up and glared as the three men entered, but no one spoke.

"They don't look too happy, do they?" said Durken, gently pulling back his duster to put his Colt within reach.

"Nope." McAfee took a last puff on his cigarette, dropped it in the sawdust at his feet, and ground it out with his heel.

A man pushed himself from the bar and stood upright. "What are you going to do about this, Parker?" The speaker was a short fellow dressed in range clothes with a low-slung holstered Colt. "We aren't just going to wait around here to die. We want out."

"From what I see, the Army won't let you go, Jack. My authority only goes so far, and it doesn't reach over the U.S. government."

"That's what you say," growled a big man in overalls wearing a gun belt slung across his chest like a bandolier and a hat with a caved in crown.

"They have orders to shoot us," said Jack. "Maybe we ought to shoot a few of them."

Parker crossed the floor to stand face to face with Jack and without warning, punched him square in the chin and knocked him flat. Jack's eyes rolled back in his head and he lay still. Some of the men started toward Parker, but Durken and McAfee already had their guns out, and in a second, so did Parker.

"Now listen to me, all of you. You're mad, and you're scared, and you're liquored up, and that's a bad mix. You're farmers and cowboys. You think you're going to go march down the road and face off against men who kill for a living? I'll tell you what'll happen. You'll die now instead of maybe living 'til tomorrow."

The mob grew suddenly silent. Parker stepped away from Jack, and none of his friends came forward to pick him up. "Now," said Parker, "somebody tell me who's in charge of the Army unit and where I can find him."

"Name's Dobbs," said a voice from behind them. "Lieutenant Dobbs, and I'm right here." Dobbs was flanked by a pair of soldiers, rifles at the ready.

Introductions were made and everyone relaxed a little and put their guns aside. "We need to talk. Let's get away from this mob." Dobbs gestured toward the crowd along the bar.

"Good idea," said Parker. "They probably shouldn't be listening in while we sort this out, anyway."

They left the saloon and Dobbs led them to the telegraph office. The men went inside, as the two soldiers took posts flanking the doorway. A corporal sat at the telegraph key, his pistol on the table beside it.

Dobbs sank heavily into a chair, took off his hat, and set it on the table in front of him. "That business in the saloon's pretty much how the town's attitude's been for the past twenty-four hours."

"Can't say I blame the townspeople for being spooked," Parker said, "and up to now, it's all hearsay. If they'd've seen what the three of us have, there'd be a full-bore panic."

"What I've seen's bad enough," Dobbs replied. "To make things worse, a bunch of the local folks heard the explosion and hurried out there to see what was going on."

"Explosion?" said McAfee. "Cullison set off the charges? Sealed the cave?"

"There's no cave there anymore that we could see. But as to whether the snakes attacked before or after, it's hard to tell." He shuddered. "I've seen battlefields and massacres, people scalped, heads blown off, bodies torn in half, and I've never seen anything so gruesome as what those snakes did to Cullison and his men. We were ordered to leave them above ground. Right now they're wrapped in blankets treated with camphor and laid out on the floor of a barn at the edge of town. I'd high-tail it out of here right now if I didn't have orders to stay and contain the civilians."

"Why keep them here?" Parker's tone was sharper than a simple question called for.

"Because they saw it. What the snakes did. We let them go, word'll spread like wildfire all up and down the territories. The politicals are afraid of a panic."

"This keeps up much longer, that horse'll be out of the barn anyway."

"You're probably right, but in the meantime, I have to follow orders."

"The Grand Design," McAfee said, slowly shaking his head. "Manifest Destiny. Can't let anything get in the way."

"I don't know anything about all that," said Dobbs. "All I do know is I'm about as jumpy as those boys in the saloon. What can you tell me about this I don't know already?"

For the next half hour, Durken, McAfee, and Parker recounted the events that brought them back to Casselman. "So this Tate's behind us keeping these people here?"

"He's just following orders like the rest of us, I suppose, Dobbs." Durken leaned back in his chair and fished for his tobacco. "He just seems a little freer with the interpretation."

"I don't like it," Dobbs said, shaking his head. "Orders are orders, but I hate to think about having my men shoot civilians. They had to shoot one, and even that's more than I signed up for."

"None of us likes it, Dobbs," said McAfee. "What about that piece of the Constitution that says the sheriff has authority over all other enforcement? And *posse comitatus* while we're on the subject?"

"That might be true in Nevada since statehood, but Utah is still a territory, and apparently those laws don't apply. No offense to you, Sheriff," Dobbs turned to Parker, "but your authority doesn't trump mine."

"Plays right into Tate's hands, don't it?" Durken said, rising from his chair. "That bastard's got it all figured out."

Dobbs rose "Right now, Sheriff, the best thing we all can do is keep these folks from panicking. You made a good start with Jack Hooley. He's been instigating trouble since we arrived."

"I noticed you didn't take their guns," said Parker.

Dobbs replied. "If we tried to do that, Sheriff, there would be bloodshed, and in good conscience, seeing what I saw, I couldn't leave those people defenseless."

"Trouble is, guns don't seem to help much," said Durken.

Dobbs nodded. "That's true, and it's all I can do to keep my men from deserting, but as long as they have a way to fight back, the townspeople still think they have hope, and we can't afford to let them think otherwise."

"Is the telegraph working?" Durken said. "We should send a message to General Sherman."

"Give it to Corporal Mayhew," Dobbs tilted his head toward the soldier at the code key. "You know what you can and can't say over the wire."

"Unfortunately," said McAfee, "Yes we do."

Durken scrawled a quick message to the General and handed it to Mayhew. "I told him where we were and that we'd arrive sometime tomorrow."

"Good enough." Dobbs rose from his chair. "You gentlemen will check in with me before you leave tomorrow, in case anything new comes up to tell the General."

"We'll do that," said Durken.

"I won't be leaving, Lieutenant. I'll stick around to help keep order."

"That makes me rest easier, Sheriff," said Dobbs. "A familiar face will help."

Parker went back to the saloon to keep the mob quiet while Durken and McAfee tended to the horses.

"That Dobbs is a good man in a bad situation," McAfee said, throwing Sweetheart's saddle over the side of his stall.

"Like that fellah you told me about had to sail between the whirlpool and that monster took a half dozen of his men and ate them. What's his name?"

"Odysseus. Being in command makes for some hard choices, especially when you run into something you've never seen before."

"Nobody's ever seen before," Durken added.

"Where do you want to sleep tonight?"

"Not over that saloon." Durken looked around him. Plenty of hay over there in that stall. We can bed down there."

"Sounds sensible. I'll take the first watch."

"No need. I figure the horses'll let us know if something ain't right."

"They're good for that, aren't they?"

"That's why they call it 'horse sense.'"

LIV

The rest of the night was uneventful, and with the grey dawn, the cowboys rode out of Casselman. Dobbs' adjutant, a sergeant named Wilson rode along to tell the sentries to let Durken and McAfee through. They passed two families with all their possessions piled in farm wagons, waiting and watching, a hundred yards from the blockade.

The sergeant pointed. "They've been camped out there since yesterday, ready to roll out as soon as the guard is lifted."

As the three rode by, the faces of the men, women, and children first brightened with expectation, then sank with the realization that nothing had changed, then darkened with resentment that someone else was allowed to leave but they were not. They set to shouting, and as the cowboys rode away, the sentries took up their rifles, ready for trouble.

"Damn, that makes me feel bad."

"Yep, but for all we know, Durken, if they rode ten miles down the road, the same thing could happen to them as did the Possets."

"Or to us."

"Or to us. That's why we're going and not them."

"Damn."

"Yep."

LV

Parker left Casselman shortly after Durken and McAfee did. The townspeople had settled down considerably, and Dobbs seemed to have things pretty well in hand. He arrived late that afternoon in Collinsville to find his deputies in a state of high agitation.

"Sheriff, am I glad you're back. There's a fellah here says he's kin to one of those dead men we got in the livery and he's been nagging at us to see them. I told him we didn't have any authority for that and he'd have to wait for you, but the longer he waits, the louder he gets."

"What's his name?"

"Jake Ketchum, he says."

Parker shook his head. "I figured he'd turn up before long. I just didn't think he'd get here so quick. Where is he?"

Jake Ketchum sat hunched over a corner table, his forearms on either side of a bottle of whiskey and a glass tumbler as if to prevent someone from snatching them away from him. Yes, he'd gone back to drink, but who wouldn't with all he'd been through. How could he tell Helen her brother was dead? And now that he'd picked up the bottle again, he realized he wouldn't put it down again. She'd leave him for good, and that was just one more reason to pour another glass.

Parker walked into the saloon and saw the dusty stranger slumped in a chair. "You Ketchum?"

The head raised, and Parker saw the livid scar across the sunburned forehead. "Yeah." The bloodshot eyes struggled to focus, first on Parker's face, then on his star.

"I'm Sheriff Curtis Parker. Deputies said you wanted to see your brother's..."

"Brother-in-law," Ketchum shot back a little too quickly for as drunk as he seemed to be. "Hank Martin's my brother-in-law."

"Yes, sir. I understand. Well, if you'll come with me, you can identify the remains and we'll do whatever's appropriate."

Ketchum pushed back his chair and rocked out of it to an unsteady half crouch, hands still on the table, bracing him. He took a deep breath, and when he let it out, Parker could smell the whiskey he'd been drinking all afternoon. He took Ketchum by the elbow, but the cowboy shook off the hand. "I don't need no help." Weaving a little, he followed Parker through the doors and into the street.

In the stable, Durst and Martin were laid out on improvised tables made of planks across sawhorses. Both were wrapped in blankets. The odor of camphor was losing the battle with the stench of putrefaction. Parker lit a lantern and set it on the nearer table. "I wasn't here when they were brought in, so I can't say which is which. We'll have to unwrap them. He pulled back the corner of one blanket, revealing a grey face framed with a fringe of rusty hair.

"That looks like Durst." Ketchum wished he'd brought the bottle with him.

Parker peeled back the blanket from the second corpse revealing a head with a thick moustache. "It's Hank." Ketchum reached to pull the blanket down further and Parker grabbed his wrist.

"You oughtn't do that, Ketchum. It's a bit unpleasant."

Ketchum snarled and shoved Parker away. He pulled the cover aside and saw a mound of raw entrails. Ketchum swooned. He grabbed the table to steady himself as the afternoon's whiskey came burning back up his gullet to spill on the hay-strewn floor. Parker came up behind him and took him by the shoulders.

"What happened to him?"

"Mister Ketchum," Parker said in as even a voice as he could muster, "we'll talk about that in a little while. For now, let's cover these men back up and go to my office."

Ketchum didn't hear Parker. He was too busy staring at Martin's body. "He moved!" Ketchum pointed at the gory mound of flesh and said in a hoarse whisper, "He moved."

Parker reached around Ketchum to pull the blanket over the corpse when he saw the mass of intestines twitch. Before he could pull back his hand, a fanged head burst from the body and sank its teeth into Parker's wrist. He spun away, dragging the gore covered snake with him and knocked over the lantern, which burst on the floor, catching the hay afire.

Ketchum, still holding onto the table, opened his mouth to scream, but another snake struck from Martin's entrails, its thrust taking it through his lips, to clamp venomous jaws on his tongue. He sank to the floor, the venom burning his mouth and the flames burning his back. His last thought was that someone else would have to face Helen.

LVI

The General's train stood at the siding, the engine occasionally chuffing as it maintained steam, like a horse standing in a carriage harness blowing air, waiting for the flick of the driver's whip. The sentries came to attention as Durken and McAfee rode up.

In the late afternoon sun, the General's car stood glazed by a fine drizzle that was just letting up. A faint trace of a rainbow arched over the plain to the east.

"Seems we always have one more stop before going home." Durken shook droplets of water from his hat.

"Kinda like Purgatory."

They dismounted, and McAfee said, "Lieutenants Durken and McAfee reporting to General Sherman."

The sentries saluted and the one to the left said, "Yes, sir. Please wait here a moment." He climbed the steps to the platform and rapped on the door of the car. A tall man, hatless, but wearing a second lieutenant's bars, came out. "Come up, men. The General is expecting you."

Sherman sat behind the table piled with papers, looking, as he often did, as if he hadn't shaved or slept for days. His white shirt was undone, revealing the buttons of his union suit underneath it. In one hand he held a telegram and the other a cigar.

"Men, this is my adjutant, Lieutenant Hobson. You may speak freely in his presence."

Durken and McAfee looked at each other as if to say, where do we start? McAfee began recounting events since he had last met with Sherman, and Durken chimed in as events included him. When they reached the end of the story, Sherman stared at the telegram he'd been holding the entire time.

"Colbert and his men are dead in Mannville. Snakes."

"What about Tate and Black and Willoughby?"

"Black and Willoughby are dead. Tate is missing. I know you two resented being pulled away from this operation, but it seems in one way, at least, it was a blessing. Live to fight another day."

"I have to ask, General," said Durken, "What will happen to those folks in Casselman? The Army can't keep them prisoners forever."

"That, I regret to say, is out of my hands. But I will exert whatever influence I have to see that they will ultimately be treated in a humane fashion. On that, you have my word."

"And Tate?"

"The Secret Service can hunt him down, dead or alive, makes no difference to me. Let the Devil take care of his own, I say."

"And what happens now, sir?" said McAfee.

"Now, I follow the orders I was given and decommission the pair of you and you go back to being cowboys. If I had my way, you'd be headed back to Mannville in five minutes, but I can't buck Washington." He sighed heavily. "You've heard me say it before. An Army is a collection of armed men obliged to obey one man. Every change in the rules which impairs the principle weakens the army. And that I will not advocate. Hobson?"

The lieutenant handed each of the cowboys a sheet of paper signed in Sherman's slanted hand. The essence of the orders was that effective immediately, Durken and McAfee were civilians again.

Sherman reached for the bottle of whiskey at the corner of the table. "Hobson, bring glasses for these men, and while you're at it, bring one for yourself as well. We all deserve a drink."

As McAfee and Durken rode away, Sherman stepped out onto the platform of the car and watched them shrink into the horizon. "If I had fifty men like those two, Hobson, we could all go home in a week."

LVII

"This ain't over, you know?" Durken said as they turned onto the road leading to the Triple Six.

"No, it's not. We need to talk to Seven Stars."

"Yep, but first, I need a bath and a shave and a decent meal."

"I think there's enough time for that."

The sun had just set by the time they rode through the gateway to the ranch.

"Looks just like we left it."

"Yep," said Durken. "Wilcox must've done a proper job."

The horses were all in the stable, and across the yard, they could see cowboys walking toward the bunkhouse where Charlie would be cooking a hearty supper for the ranch hands. A few early lights shone in the windows of the Mansion and smoke curled from the kitchen chimney at the back of the big house.

"It feels strange riding in here after the last few days," said McAfee. "Like waking up after a bad dream."

"I can't say I'm sorry to be back. I just feel like they pulled us off the horse before it was broke."

"What did Colbert say? That they'd finish it? I guess not."

At that moment, a square of light appeared at the front of the mansion as the door was flung wide, and a figure ran from the doorway, across the porch, and into the yard. McAfee jumped down from Sweetheart and started toward Sarah.

"Tell you what," Durken chuckled, "I'll see to the horses while you tend to other matters." He took Sweetheart's reins in one hand and clucked his tongue. Thunder took the lead, and both horses ambled toward the stable where they'd find hay, water, and rest.

He was hanging up the bridles when McAfee came into the stable. "Guess who wants to talk to us."

"No guess necessary. I guess we don't have time to get a bath and a shave, do we."

McAfee shook his head. "Nope. Eldridge said, 'immediately.'"

"Well, I suppose if Miss Sarah can tolerate your stink, delicate as she is, I suppose her daddy can manage the two of us."

"Now that I think about it, I kinda like the idea of stinking up that study of his."

Durken laughed. "If he lights up one of stogies he favors, he won't know the difference."

Once the horses were bedded, the cowboys headed for the Mansion.

"We better go around back," Durken said. "Don't want to track manure on that fancy French rug in the entrance."

Now it was McAfee's turn to laugh. "You don't fool me one bit. There's another attraction to going in the kitchen door. She has red hair, unless it turned white the last week worrying about you."

Durken grinned. "Guilty as charged."

Maggie was waiting in the doorway, hands on hips, when they came around the corner to the back porch. "So ye're back, the two of you. And neither of you in a sling or on a travois. Do miracles never cease?"

"Happy to see you too, Maggie," said McAfee, putting a finger to the brim of his hat as he crossed the porch. Durken hung back at the foot of the back steps as McAfee squeezed past Maggie. "I'll tell Mister Eldridge you'll be along directly, seeing as how your bad leg still slows you down a little." He disappeared into the house and left the pair alone.

Durken took off his hat and held it by the brim in his fingers. "Hullo, Maggie. Told you I'd be back."

"I had a whole mindful of things to say to you, to give you what for, and now, I can't…I can't…" She started to cry.

"Aw, Maggie." Durken hobbled up the steps and took her in his arms. She buried her face in his chest and shook with sobs. He held her until the crying subsided and then she pushed away from him. "Go on. Himself is waiting for you." She turned on her heel and started through the door then turned back. "And wipe your muddy boots, you spalpeen. I just mopped the floor."

Durken sighed with relief at the thought that suddenly Maggie was herself again.

He limped down the hallway to the closed door of Eldridge's study and though he couldn't make out the actual words, the tone of Eldridge's voice was clear. He opened the door without knocking and Eldridge stopped abruptly. He glared at Durken. "Well, now that we're all here, maybe we can accomplish something."

Durken took a chair beside McAfee, who sat with his hat on his knee.

"Looks just like we left it."

As always, Durken left his on his head. If Eldridge told him specifically to remove it, he would have, but he wasn't one for manners toward the undeserving.

"As I was just telling McAfee here," Eldridge said, annoyance apparent in his voice, "we have to get ready to drive five hundred head of cattle to Reno by the sixteenth. I assume your leg is well enough to make the trip?"

"I'll manage."

Eldridge frowned as if he were disappointed at the news and had one less complaint, but that didn't stop him from reciting a litany of them.

"Did Wilcox do all right managing things?" McAfee asked.

"He was," Eldridge paused, searching for a word that wasn't too complimentary, "adequate."

"I figured he would be."

"Now about the drive to Reno…"

A few minutes later as they crossed the yard toward the bunkhouse, Durken turned to McAfee and said, "I wonder why he doesn't just fire us if he's so dissatisfied with things."

"He can't do that because that'd break the rules of the game he plays."

"Game?"

"He's not a third the man either of us is. In his heart he knows it, but he wants to prove to himself that isn't so. He orders us around and it makes him feel more powerful. If he fires us, he's admitting defeat. He has to make us quit to show he's the better man 'cause he held out longer."

"And neither of us is of that mind."

"Nope. After all the guff I took in the Army, there isn't much that Eldridge could say or do to upset me. And you seem to have fun irritating him."

"You have to admit it: you enjoy it as much as I do."

"Most days."

"We're going to have to go visit Seven Stars."

"Yeah, but we'd better do it on our own time, maybe tomorrow after supper."

As they neared the bunkhouse, the aroma of Charlie's stew grew stronger and the raucous laughter and banter of the cowboys at table grew louder. "I hope there's enough stew left for both of us," Durken said. "I'd hate to have to shoot you over the last bowl."

"Priorities."

"Yep."

LVIII

The next day, the cowboys fell back into the rhythm of the ranch as if they'd never left. Wilcox gratefully gave the job of running things back to them, saying, "You're welcome to it. There ain't enough silver in Nevada to make me take over again."

Durken's leg was pretty well healed, and he had little trouble climbing into Thunder's saddle. The wound no longer throbbed when he rode. "Charlie's poultices work better than the doc's pills. I'm just about back to my old self."

"Yeah, if I'm going to outrun you in a foot race, it better be soon."

While Slye and Smeck rode the fence line, Durken and McAfee supervised the herd count. Wilcox and Bailey looked for strays.

"There's a lot of merit to a regular life," McAfee said, wiping his brow with his kerchief.

"Yeah, that's so," Durken replied, "but not nearly as interesting."

"You know, there's an old Chinese curse: 'May you live in interesting times.'"

"You read that in some book?"

"No, Charlie told me."

"Well, coming back to our life here, I can't say as I feel cursed."

"Better to be out of that business."

"You really mean that?"

"A year ago, I would've said no, but now I'm not so sure."

"If the General sends for us, we going back?"

"Probably so."

"Old habits die hard."

"Yep."

After supper, Durken rode through the gate and aimed Thunder to the north and the Monatai village. McAfee hung back to spend a few quiet moments with Miss Sarah, but he would catch up along the way.

The night air was cool, and overhead, the stars sparkled like tiny shards of a broken bottle. Durken knew as well as McAfee did that the Snake Mother was still out there somewhere over the horizon, and as long as she was, he couldn't rest easy any more than McAfee or the General could.

The waning moon threw enough light to keep the trail in sight for the moment, but it would likely set before they got back to the ranch. Maybe they could stay in the Monatai village until first light and ride back in time to start work. The horses knew the way, but Durken didn't like the thought of riding back in darkness.

He and McAfee had faced a lot of enemies, human and otherwise, in the war and after, but dealing with the snakes bothered him like nothing before. If it weren't for their respect and devotion to the General, neither of them would willingly have gone on some of the missions they had. This time…

His thoughts were interrupted by the sound of hooves behind him at a quick trot. "Don't shoot, Durken; it's me." Durken turned to see McAfee on Sweetheart closing the distance between them.

"All the more reason."

McAfee pulled alongside and slowed Sweetheart's pace to match Thunder's.

"So, did you and Miss Sarah have your *tête-à-tête*?

McAfee whistled. "I guess hanging around me's improved your vocabulary after all." He chuckled. "Yeah, she's glad I'm back, I can tell you that."

"And so are we."

"No argument there."

Neither said much until the bluff that protected the Monatai village came into view. McAfee began an off-key whistle of "Red River Valley" to let the brave on guard knew they were coming openly and not sneaking up on the village.

When they reached the foot of the bluff, a voice called out, "Durken and McAfee."

"Is that you, Brave Bear?"

"It is."

"You got some sharp eyes on you in this light," Durken said.

"Sharp ears," said the brave. "McAfee's whistle, once heard, is never forgotten."

Both the cowboys laughed, and McAfee said, "We come to see Seven Stars."

"Enter as friends."

In the village, a brave took their horses as they dismounted, and they were led to Seven Stars' tent at the end of the village. From within, Seven Stars said, "Friend Durken. Your leg is healing, and McAfee joins you. Welcome. Please enter, my friends."

"Thank you. Seven Stars," said McAfee.

"Much obliged," Durken added.

The inside of the tent was dim. A low fire burned in the pit in the center. The chief sat cross legged on a mound of buffalo skins, a large book in his lap. Looking closely, McAfee recognized it as the Braille Bible Seven Stars had been given a year before. "Please, put some wood on the fire. I need no light to read, but you are not as comfortable with the darkness as I." He touched the leather band that covered his missing eyes. His smile faded. "Please, sit. Tell me, what has come of your search for the Tonapa?"

"Well," Duken began, "we didn't exactly find them but…" For the next half hour as the fire crackled and the smoke curled through the hole at the wigwam's peak, the cowboys recounted for the second time in as many days, the tale of their truncated mission. The more they told Seven Stars, the deeper the lines in his face grew. When they finished, no one spoke for a time. Finally Seven Stars broke the silence.

"Your story troubles me greatly. I had believed that Ki-No Na-Te would not trouble this world again, but I am proven wrong. She cannot cross the Shadowlands between worlds, but she can inhabit a willing host if she is summoned by someone who performs great magic."

"You say inhabit," McAfee leaned forward. "Like demon possession, right?"

Seven Stars shook his head. "Far more than that. Ki-No- Na-Te can take not only the mind, but the body and transform it to her needs. The inhabited soul becomes the goddess in every way."

"A Lamia," McAfee breathed.

"Yes," Seven Stars replied, "Lamia, Echidna, Gorgon, or Lilith, she is known by many names in many places where men have summoned her. A powerful shaman is at work here, one who knows the ancient ways, and who is willing to bring the kind of destruction only Ki-No Na-Te can cause. She can be killed because at root she is human, but the shaman would only find another host. The only way to stop the evil is to find this sorcerer, destroy him, or her, and all who follow that path."

"So the danger is still out there," McAfee said.

"Yes. I can only hope that your Army is able to stop it."

"But you have your doubts," Durken added.

"I regret that I do." He was silent a moment, then said, "The hour is late. Please accept my village's hospitality for the night. Friends such as you are always welcome."

LIX

Before dawn, McAfee and Durken saddled their horses and rode out of the Monatai village. The stars were still out and the moon had set, so they rode more slowly than usual, waiting for the glow of dawn.

"You know, the biggest problem with the Tonapa and the Snake Mother is that they strike without warning and go hole up again and leave everybody scratching their heads wondering where to look for them."

McAfee replied, "That's the hell of it. We have to wait for them to act before we can do anything about it."

"Maybe that's not all true. There are some things we can do. We can clean out any caves or mines around here, make sure the Tonapa haven't set up shop in them."

"Yeah, but when? Sunday afternoons after services?" McAfee shook his head. "We got jobs. And we'd need help. Can you imagine going to Homer Eldridge and saying, 'We can't tell you why, but we need to borrow the crew for a week or two.' And we couldn't tell the men what we're after either, 'cause we're sworn to secrecy."

"You're right. And it wouldn't be fair to take them into the fight not knowing what they were fighting. We saw how that worked out with Tate." Durken spat. "Wonder what happened to him."

"Maybe the snakes ate him for supper," McAfee said with a chuckle. "They did, they'd've all died of indigestion. That would've solved a lot of problems."

"Somehow, I can't quite believe that's how it went."

"Me either."

Ahead of the sun, the sky was a shade of pale rose dotted with deep purple clouds.

"'Rosy fingered dawn,'" McAfee said.

"Yep. Always meant trouble for that Odysseus fellow, didn't it?"

"Did I ever tell you that the Roman name for Odysseus was Ulysses?"

"No kidding? Just like Grant. I guess that fits, seeing as how both were commanders."

"One big difference: when Odysseus came home from the war, he took up weapons to clean his own house. The President can't seem to get around to it."

"And that," said Durken, "gives us people like Tate and the Secret Service."

"Just like snakes in a cave."

And that was pretty much all the conversation that passed between them until they got to the Triple Six.

The day passed without incident, if you discount Smeck's horse stepping in a prairie dog hole and throwing him. Smeck's leg was broken, but as Durken observed, "Better Smeck than the horse. We'd have to shoot the horse, and that would be a loss."

After supper, the cowboys crossed the yard to the Mansion. Things were shaping up for the drive to Reno, and Eldridge wanted to put his stamp on every detail.

"Never seen a man puts his fingers in so much but never gets them dirty," McAfee said.

"Me either."

They walked around back and through the kitchen where Maggie was pumping water into a kettle. As they came through the door, she wiped away a strand of hair that was plastered by sweat to her forehead.

"Hullo, Maggie," Durken said, and added, "Nobody's ever going to fault you for industry."

"Well, if you were a gentleman, you'd come over here and pump the water for me."

"Sorry, Maggie; can't do that. We don't dare keep Eldridge waiting, now do we?"

"Aaah, get on with ye," she said, waving them away, and turning her head so that Durken couldn't see the amused smile that crossed her face.

Down the hallway, the cowboys stopped at Eldridge's door. McAfee was about to knock when Durken said, "Into the lion's den again."

"Take a deep breath." Both knew that in Eldridge's study, a report that should take ten minutes would drag past a half hour because Eldridge would interrupt every other sentence asking questions and carping at the answers.

McAfee knocked and opened the door without waiting for an invitation. He stood to the side, one arm across his stomach and the other extended in deference. "After you, 'podner.'"

LX

Sarah was sitting on the green silk divan in the parlor reading a book of Shakespeare's sonnets and listening for the door of her father's study to open so that she could just happen by and steal a few moments with

McAfee. "'My mistress' eyes are nothing like the sun,'" she read aloud and repeated the verse, slowly. What did Shakespeare mean? Clarence knew a lot about poetry and he'd read Shakespeare. She'd have to ask him.

Her reverie was interrupted by a knock at the front door. She got up from the sofa and headed into the foyer to answer it. Sarah unlocked the door. Before she could open it, Maggie, lamp in hand, came up behind her, reached over her shoulder, and slipped the chain latch into place. "It's night, Miss, and we don't know who might be about at this hour."

Sarah opened the door the few inches the chain would allow. A man stood on the porch, a man in a tattered suit and a derby hat. His head was down as if he were studying his dusty shoes.

"Yes?" Sarah said, peering through the gap in the doorway for a better glimpse of the visitor.

The stranger spoke slowly, as if measuring every syllable. "I am Special Agent Tate. I am looking for Durken and McAfee." He raised his head to look into Sarah's face, and she screamed at the sight of the agent's diamond pupils.

Tate tried to push into the doorway, but Maggie threw her weight against the door and slammed it, knocking Tate backward, but not before Sarah saw the dark shape that rose on the shadowed porch behind him.

Sarah's scream stopped Eldridge's fist halfway to his desk. "What the devil?"

McAfee sprang to his feet and ran into the hallway with Durken close behind him. Sarah was hysterical. "That man," she babbled. "His eyes, his eyes."

The front door rattled in its frame as a powerful body slammed against it.

"What the hell's going on?" Eldridge had come out of his study and stood in the hallway.

Durken took Maggie by the shoulders. "Take Miss Sarah and get upstairs. Lock yourselves in a room and stay there."

The door rattled under another blow.

"But what...?"

Durken's eyes blazed. "God damn it, Maggie, just do it!" His shout galvanized her and she took the frightened Sarah's arm in both hands and half dragged her up the staircase.

"You know what's out there, don't you?" McAfee said.

"Got a good notion." Durken pulled his Colt and fanned three shots through the door. Another blow shook the whole house.

"I got an idea." McAfee ran up the staircase

"Eldridge," shouted Durken, "shotguns. We need shotguns."

Homer ran back into his study. He grabbed shotguns from their wall mounts, filigreed double-barrels, fancy over-unders, and piled them on his desk. Then he scrabbled through a cabinet across the room, looking for shells.

Upstairs, Maggie drew a curtain away from the window of Sarah's bedroom. She stared down at the moonlit yard and crossed herself. "Saints protect us," she gasped.

"What is it, Maggie? What do you see?"

Sarah ran to the window, but Maggie blocked her path. She put her arms around the hysterical girl and held her in a tight embrace. "Better you not see, child. Better you not see."

Another blow struck the door. This time Durken could hear the oaken frame cracking. He fired through the door again. It wouldn't hold much longer. "Eldridge! Where are those guns?"

Before Homer could answer, the door burst from its hinges and fell flat into the foyer. Durken jumped backward and collided with Eldridge who had come up behind him with an armload of long guns. Eldridge went over backwards and the guns spilled in every direction.

For a second, Durken was transfixed by the sight of Ki-No Na-Te as the serpent woman rose to her full height in the foyer. Her golden snake eyes glittered in the lamplight, and her coppery scales gleamed like pennies at her breasts. Her mouth gaped and her forked tongue swung side to side. On her head, the mass of serpents swayed angrily like willow branches in a windstorm.

Durken scooped up a double-barreled shotgun from the floor and pulled both triggers. The impact knocked the lamia backward and peppered her breast with bloody wounds, but in a second, she recovered, dragging her coils through the doorway behind her.

"Get back!" McAfee shouted from the top of the stairs. At the sound of his voice, Durken turned to see his friend clanking down the staircase in the full suit of armor and holding the broadsword in his mailed fists.

The Snake Mother saw the new enemy and before McAfee could reach the bottom of the stairs, she slithered at him in attack. McAfee swung the sword overhead two-handed, and its edge caught the lamia's hand. Her clawed fingers flew across the room, and blood spattered as she jerked the hand back. She hissed in pain. The huge rattle at the end of her tail chattered like pebbles in a tin can. The goddess swung her remaining claws at McAfee and they glanced off the armor, ineffective.

McAfee pressed his advantage and stepped to the floor of the foyer, raising the sword for another blow. The goddess whipped her coils around his legs and pulled them from beneath him. McAfee went over with a crash onto the floor, and between the heavy armor and Ki-No Na-Te's coils could not find his feet again.

By this time, Durken had picked up another shotgun and fired it this time at the lamia's head. As if she knew what was coming, her hideous head bobbed and his aim went high. The double-aught buckshot plowed through the mass of writhing snakes. Some fell limp, and some simply blew apart. Ki-No Na-Te swiped back handed at Durken and caught him across the chest with her damaged arm, throwing him halfway down the hallway.

Her jaws closed over McAfee's helmet. Her fangs couldn't penetrate the steel, but as McAfee watched through the slits in the visor, he saw the serpent's tongue working over the openings. The slime from her tongue dripped onto his face, and McAfee felt his will to fight slowly drifting away like an unmoored skiff.

Durken picked up another gun and ran at the monster. He shoved the barrels into the notch where her neck met her shoulder and pulled the triggers. Blood and bits of flesh sprayed the wallpaper. The serpent woman's head hung to the side, but she was not dead. Her hand shot out and her claws closed on Durken's throat, lifting him off the floor.

Another shotgun roared, and the light went out of the diamond eyes. The Snake Mother's head rolled from her shoulders and fell to the floor. The claws let go of Durken and he fell beside the monster's head. One of the last of its snakes reared up to strike him but fell limp.

A blood-covered Homer Eldridge stood, ashen faced with shock, clutching a smoking over-under shotgun. Durken stood and limped to the doorway. He stared across the yard and said, "Eldridge, help McAfee up. We got another problem."

Across the yard in the light of the rising moon, Durken saw the ancient shaman and his followers, and behind them, the ground dark with snakes. From the gateway came the keening chant, and the mass of snakes surged forward.

Rifle fire sounded from the bunkhouse. The crew didn't know what the shooting was all about but reckoned that gunfire and Indians meant trouble. The braves clustered around the shaman as they had before, and took the bullets, some of the injured holding up the bodies of the dead as shields for their master.

Durken hobbled into the parlor. His leg was wet with blood, and he realized that his wound had opened again; either that or her had a new one. He took a lamp from the end tables in either hand and started through the door.

"What are you going to do with those?" Eldridge blurted.

"Set fire to the porch."

"What? Why the hell are you doing that?"

"Look for yourself." Durken pointed across the yard to the mass of snakes flowing like a wave in the moonlight across a hundred yards of empty space. He unscrewed the bases of the lamps and poured a line of kerosene across the porch and dumped the rest on the steps. The hissing and chattering of the rattlesnakes was growing louder. Durken fumbled for a match and realized that his bleeding wound had soaked the ones in his pocket.

He broke the top of one of the lamps, exposing the still smoldering wick. He held the glowing edge to the kerosene but it wasn't enough to light the fire. "Eldridge! Get matches or anything burning!"

Eldridge came running with a handful of matches. Durken struck one and was about to light the kerosene when he heard another sound, like a rushing wind overtaking the hissing of the snakes. The moon grew dark, eclipsed for a moment, then grew bright again as the dark shapes of birds, eagles, hawks, crows, swept down on the snakes, seizing them in their beaks and flying away until none were left.

McAfee, joined Durken and Eldridge on the porch in time to see a pair of birds like winged men swoop down and grasp the shaman in their talons. They carried him screaming high into the air and dropped him to the hard-packed earth where his body burst apart in a gory spray of entrails.

On a bluff a half mile from the ranch, Seven Stars turned to Grey Raven. "It is finished?"

Grey Raven nodded, then remembered that his chief was blind. "Yes, Seven Stars." He added. "For the moment."

LXI

The next day, swirling murders of crows led Durken and McAfee to a canyon where they found the broken bodies of uncountable rattlesnakes, dropped from such a height by the defending birds that their bodies burst and bones shattered on the rocks. The crows covered the ground like an ebony blanket, pecking the flesh from the dead invaders.

"Never seen anything like it," said Durken.

"'And I saw an angel standing in the sun; and he cried out in a loud voice, saying to all the fowls that fly in the midst of heaven, "Come and gather yourselves together unto the supper of the great God."'"

"Which book is that one from?"

"Revelation."

"Funny, I never figured Seven Stars for an angel."

"I suppose people never do recognize them in the thick of things; only afterward."

"What do we do about Special Agent Tate?" said Durken.

They found the agent on the porch, unconscious, knocked aside by the Snake Mother as she battered the door of the Mansion. The crew bound him hand and foot, locked him in a root cellar, and put a guard at the door. For a while, he'd scream a lot of gibberish about killing everyone, then he'd quiet down a while then start right in again. So far, the men hadn't so much as opened the cellar door.

"I'd like to bring him out here and let the crows have him."

"Me too, but I don't think we could get away with that."

"Probably not." Durken stroked his chin. "I say we leave him trussed up, throw him in the buckboard, and deliver him to the General. He'll know what to do with him."

"What if the General's pulled out of Bacon Rock?"

"Put Tate in a sack, throw him in a freight car and send him whichever way the General went."

McAfee nodded. "Sounds like a sensible plan."

They turned the horses and started back to the Triple Six.

"I bet the next time the General sends us on a mission Eldridge won't grouse about it so much, now that he knows the kinds of things we're fighting. Maggie or Sarah, either."

"I hate to admit it," Durken said, "but Eldridge did his share."

"No surprise. Man does a lot he wouldn't do otherwise when something threatens his hearth and home."

"Think we'll ever be in that spot?"

"A year ago, I would have said no straightaway. Now, I'm not so sure."

"Me either."

"How's your leg?"

"Hurts."

"There's a cure for that." McAfee grinned. "Race you to the Silver Dollar. Loser buys."

Durken shouted "Hut!" Thunder and Sweetheart took off at a gallop, and the cowboys chased their shadows all the way to Bacon Rock.

THE END

ABOUT OUR CREATORS

AUTHOR —

FRED ADAMS–is a western Pennsylvania native who has enjoyed a lifelong love affair with horror, fantasy, and science fiction literature and films. He holds a Ph.D. in American Literature from Duquesne University and recently retired from teaching writing and literature in the English Department of Penn State University.

He has published over 50 short stories in amateur, and professional magazines as well as hundreds of news features as a staff writer and sportswriter for the now Pittsburgh Tribune-Review. In the 1970s Fred published the fanzine Spoor and its companion The Spoor Anthology. *Hitwolf, Six-Gun Terrors* and *Dead Man's Melody* (nominated Year's Best Pulp Novel 2017 Pulp Factory Awards) were his three first books for Airship 27, all of which have become series.

INTERIOR ILLUSTRATOR—

ART COOPER–is a Canadian artist/writer/editor who was a found partner of Spectrum Publications, which published bi-monthly fanzines in the early 70s. Art was a member of the inaugural Cartooning program at Sheridan College in Oakville, Ontario, where the guest instructors included such luminaries as Joe Kubert, Neal Adams and Will Eisner. Art contributed to a number of fan publications and penciled two stories for Orb Magazine before getting married and completing his engineering degree. Art has worked as a project manager in the Mining and Metals industry for the past few decades, and has done some freelance advertising work on the side. Art is the proud father of two grown sons and lives in Mississauga, Ontario with his current wife and daughter.

COVER ARTIST—

TED HAMMOND–is a Canadian artist who has been creating amazing art for over twenty years. His work has appeared in magazines, ads, books and graphic novels just to name a few. Go to (www.tedhammond.com) to contact him and check out more of his work!

More books from Fred Adams Jr.:

SIX-GUN TERRORS Vol One
SIX-GUN TERRORS Vol Two

HITWOLF
HITWOLF – The Pack

C.O. JONES
C.O. JONES – Skinners

(SAM DUNNE MYSTERIES)
DEAD MAN'S MELODY

(THE SMITH BROTHERS)
THE EYE OF QUANG CHI

MORE FROM THE SAME AUTHOR:

THE WAYS OF MAGIC

During World War II, C.O. Jones, under a different name, was recruited into a special unit of the OSS (Office of Strategic Services). Special in that all the members had some kind of extrasensory abilities bordering on magic. Their main mission was to seek out and combat the Nazis' top secret Occult Practioners.

But the war is now over and C.O. is just another veteran looking for a fresh start. He hopes the quiet little town of Brownsville, Pennsylvania is the perfect place to do so. That is, until he gets involved with the local criminal element and discovers, through his own unique gifts, that someone is using dark magic to further their own illegal agenda. For C.O. Jones, it seems the ways of magic are to be found in the most unlikely placesone of the toughest new pulp heroes of them all.

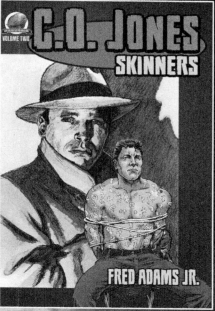

HOLLYWOOD MONSTERS

It's 1949 and army veteran C.O. Jones is living in Los Angeles working as a private investigator. When he's hired to find a missing starlet, he soon finds himself embroiled in a sophisticated conspiracy which not only includes kidnapping but high profile blackmail as well.

All of which would be enough to keep any honest, hardworking P.I. busy but when it's Jones, there is also the added element of magic to consider. Possessing an uncanny ability to recognize arcane abilities in others, Jones begins to uncover even deadlier shadows in the background. Never mind one of them may actually be a real werewolf with his own personal interest in the case.

With C.O. Jones, often times the monsters aren't only up on the big silver screen.

PULP FICTION FOR A NEW GENERATION!
THIS AND OTHER FINE READING AVAILABLE AT: AIRSHIP27HANGAR.COM

Printed in Great Britain
by Amazon

78936511R00098